Trigger Warnings

I started writing NeurodiVeRse after I came out as non-binary at my previous place of employment. The response was concerning. I was working in one of the most liberal states and a city well known for its LGBTQIA+ culture, and had some horrific experiences.

At the same time, the world was bouncing back from a pandemic with a strong push for "normality." As an autistic person, this felt like being forced to give up a calm and positive space so non-autistic people could be happier. Knowing that there were other options, many neurodiverse people refused to go back. One day, I was having a conversation with my youngest, who is also autistic. We were determining the best way for them to move forward. I asked them to describe their ideal school, and they told me about a virtual reality institution allowing them to learn at their own pace. That conversation turned into this book.

This is a work of fiction based on real lived experiences that were readapted into new situations. As unreal as you think these situations are, they happen all the time.

NeurodiVerRse Contains:

Deadnaming

Misgendering

Transphobia

Ableism

Parental Abandonment

Domestic Terrorism

Idiotic politicians

Offscreen rape and death of children

In-Between

The Immortal Part of Myself

NEURODIVERSE

MJ JAMES

Mrs. Bricker.
Sometimes teachers save lives.

To all the teachers who pay
attention to the "weird" kid.

Chapter One

Jupiter J'naii's phone alarm went off, the pestering sound vibrating next to the pillow where it had dropped the night before. Jupiter randomly poked at the screen until it stopped making noise, and then they put the pillow over their head, trying to shelter themselves from the day.

The next alarm started up less than five minutes later. It was set on their tablet, left in the living room the night prior. Its thud was a distant noise that they tried to ignore. But once they heard it, they couldn't unhear it, so they removed the pillow and yelled at the phone's virtual assistant to shut it off. They almost got up then, ready to start the day. Then they thought better of it, placed the pillow back on their head, and went back to sleep.

Fifteen minutes later, another alarm went off. It was set on a battery-powered alarm clock, purchased after Jupiter had missed a class in college, all because they had forgotten to charge their devices. Now it was the alarm to let them know they should be dressed and working on breakfast. It emitted a lulling steady tone that made it easy to ignore, and Jupiter returned to sleep.

The last alarm clock was plugged into the wall and was purchased after they arrived late to work. After an hour-long lecture about professionalism, they headed to the store after their workday and picked up the worst alarm clock they could find. They had plugged it into the kitchen and set it to loudly play a morning radio show. If they didn't get up and turn it off, their neighbor would soon start pounding on their wall, and the last thing they wanted to do was to have to talk to someone.

Grudgingly they took the pillow off their face, slid their legs off the bed, and stood up. They shuffled into the kitchen, turning off the jarring radio host that was screaming about something Jupiter had no interest in. They gave themselves a few moments for their brain to recover from the noise and then tottered over to turn off the second alarm clock. The house was silent, just the way they liked it.

Jupiter looked at the time and sighed. The bus would arrive in twenty minutes. They entered their room, threw off their t-shirt, and slipped on their binder and a red and black plaid collared shirt. They glanced at the blue jeans they had slept in and decided they would be suitable for another day. Afterward, they went to the kitchen, grabbed a package of Pop-Tarts, and then went to their entertainment center to pick up their noise-canceling head-phones. They looked longingly at their gaming console, wishing they could spend the day curled up in their beanbag chair, continuing with the gaming session from last night.

With a sigh, they laced up their boots, grabbed their bag, and headed out the door.

When Jupiter first moved to Long Beach, California, they were excited. They envisioned living on the beach next to blue water and golden sand. Then they saw the price of rent for a studio apartment was more than their paycheck, and they decided living closer to their work was more practical. At least until they realized that the only way they could afford to live in the area was to share space with another human being. Instead, they found a small studio apartment that barely fit their bed and tv on the city's north side. At least their place was only a ten-minute walk to a bus stop. The bus even managed to make the trip to their work in an hour and a half, even though the same journey by car only took twenty minutes.

Jupiter threw on their headphones to drown out the noise of the city. Before moving here, they had no idea people could be so loud. Or that so many people could live so close together. As they walked down the sidewalk, their eyes focused on their feet. They just managed to miss running into a child dressed in a bright red collared shirt and tan slacks. Another child stood nearby, blocking the sidewalk while their parents opened the door to one of the many cars parked bumper to bumper on the side of the road. It was enough to make Jupiter grateful for the cramped confines of public transportation.

But to make it to the bus, they had to navigate the children blocking their way. The youngest child looked up at them, giving a stare that was all too familiar, one that was usually followed by pointing and the question, "What are you?" They knew that the children did not mean any harm when they asked, but it did not lessen the sting or the humiliation when the parents gave concerned looks and ushered their children away.

Jupiter saw the child's mouth start to wrinkle in concern; their brow scrunched up in confusion, causing their long braided ponytail to sway. Their arm began to rise with an outstretched finger as Jupiter pushed their way between the older child and the minivan. Jupiter's backpack brushed along the side of the vehicle.

The parent said something loud enough for their muffled voice to be heard despite their earphones, but it was unclear enough that Jupiter could easily ignore it as they rushed to the end of the street. They also ignored the tears in their eyes and focused on getting to the bus stop on time.

Jupiter knew their knowledge of California was based on TV shows and movies, but since Hollywood was only a few miles away, they had assumed it was a pretty good picture. Instead, they found litter on the side of the roads, graffiti everywhere, and a dimness despite the sunshine. Everything was so close together, and people were everywhere. It should have made them happy. After all, they wanted nothing more than to connect to others, but even still, they had never felt more alone since arriving here a few months ago.

They glanced at their watch and tried to increase their pace, but they had done too much gaming and not enough exercise. Their lungs started to burn, but they reached the bus stop with minutes to spare.

Then they waited. As the minutes passed, they started to worry, the anxious dialogue collecting in their brain. *Was the bus early? Was their watch off? Were they going to be late to work yet again?* It didn't matter that the bus was late every day. They still became anxious as the minutes passed. Finally, they pulled out their phone to check the bus location on the transit app. As they did, the bus pulled into view.

It was an extended bus with an accordion plastic center to make the sharp city turns. Even with the extra space, the bus was full of morning commuters and students. At that moment, Jupiter wished they could drive a car. It isn't that they wanted to drive a car. The thought of being behind the wheel of a vehicle capable of such destruction caused their anxiety to flair. They were sure they could not drive a vehicle, especially not on the streets of Long Beach, where cars stopped so close to each other that there wasn't enough space for a human to walk through. No, what they wanted was to have the option. They wished their father had handed them the keys to the family minivan and let them practice in the supermarket parking lot, just like their older siblings had. But thinking about their family always put them in a dark space, so they quickly shut that thought up.

Instead, they shuffled up the steps, scanned their bus pass, and looked for where they could stand away from people. They found a place in the middle that had some space and stood for an eternity, trying to minimize physical contact every time the bus bounced or turned until it pulled in front of a middle school and half the bus emptied. The high schoolers were still here, but a seat opened up, and Jupiter slid into it and pulled out their phone.

They opened their current favorite mobile game. The tap role-playing game allowed them to escape from the people surrounding them without moving their hand enough to touch the person sitting beside them accidentally. They played, their earphones half on, while they listened to the automated voice that announced stops, half tuning it out until they heard the call for

Pacific Coast Highway. The stop was three before their own, but it gave them time to put the game away and fret anxiously about the appropriate time to pull the string down. Too early and they would have to get off at the earlier stop, and too late and they would miss their stop. Through trial and error, they determined the perfect time to pull for their stop was as they passed an electrical box painted purple with white flowers. As they reached up, they heard the unmistakable sound of the string being pulled. Someone else had reached out too early. Jupiter knew it didn't matter. It was better, actually. It meant they did not have to touch the cord thousands had already touched. Yet, they still felt an empty pit in their stomach that occurred every time their routine was interrupted.

But they were an adult and knew they had to deal with minor setbacks like that. The counselor, the one they had seen at the university while finishing up their second master's degree, was very big on reminding them how they were an adult who had to deal with minor setbacks. It still irritated Jupiter that she had called them minor, like changes were insignificant, and Jupiter was a child who could not tolerate trivial inconveniences. As the anger began to resurface, Jupiter took a deep breath and walked off the bus, ready to face the day.

Jupiter liked that they worked in an office building. They walked in and called for the elevator, waiting with all the other professionals in their suits and ties. There were a lot of companies in the building, but their company had an entire floor, the 15th floor. When Jupiter arrived for their first day of work and pushed the button for the 15th floor, they knew that this was a sign that this was where they belonged. Fifteen was such a beautiful number. It was divisible by five three times. Five was Jupiter's favorite number, and three was an extremely important number with significance throughout history in many different areas. This made 15 a positive number. They tried to explain this to the coworker assigned to show them around the office on their first day, but Jupiter knew the importance was lost on her.

They knew they saw the world differently. They always had. When they were in preschool, their parents were called into the office with a referral to a specialist who had diagnosed them with autism spectrum disorder. Their parents were furious. They told Jupiter the story often enough. Eventually, they realized that their child was not the same. Although they rarely used the word autism, their words were not very friendly, and Jupiter didn't like to think of them. Taking another deep breath, they stepped off the elevator and walked to their desk.

The office was full of cubicles, the walls so low that you could see people's heads over them. They were told it was to make communication more accessible and to increase teamwork. Jupiter found it loud. They kept their headphones on as they walked through the desks trying to keep a friendly smile. They had practiced it again last night, so it did not look like a skeleton's grimace. Not that Jupiter had any idea what that meant, only that Jennifer had said that the week before. Most of their colleagues kept their heads down, allowing Jupiter to walk through with minimal eye contact and head bobbing. Social interactions were exhausting.

When Jupiter sat at their desk, they removed their headphones, allowing a break from the pressure on their head. The noise of key clacking, printers printing, and the muffled voices of conversations hit them full force. *Why did the world have to be so loud?*

They put their headphones back on and started up their computer.

Jupiter loved their job. They worked for an educational software company, and they got to test the games that were geared toward autistic children. They did not have a direction when they obtained their Master's Degree in developmental psychology. They mostly just wanted to learn more about themselves. Not ready to leave school, they went back and got another master's degree in educational technology. When their advisor suggested that they focus their thesis on technology for autistic children, they jumped at the idea. Even better, that project had led to this job, a chance to break away and make it on their own. And they knew they were going to finally be able to make a difference.

They played a few more rounds of a game designed to teach autistic children social cues and then went back to their notes. Jupiter was glad that they had hired someone who was autistic to review this game. Some of the sections were horrible. There was one prompt that told autistic children that they had to allow people to hug them even if they didn't want to. Also, the language in the game was really derogatory: telling autistic children that stimming (when an autistic person moved or vocalized in a way to receive necessary sensory input) was a problem. Jupiter had been working on the game for the last two weeks and had a fifteen-page report ready to hand in to their boss tomorrow. They read it over again, making sure their points were clear and referenced. They bounced with excitement at the prospect of turning it in and winning over the approval of their boss.

Chapter Two

Jupiter's stomach rumbled, pulling them away from another round of the game. They looked down at their watch and noticed it was after one in the afternoon. They stood up and stretched, causing glances from coworkers sitting at their desks. Jupiter grabbed their wallet and headed to the lobby, where a little convenience store sold a small selection of premade food. Jupiter grabbed their regular tuna sandwich, a bag of plain chips, and a soda. They slid their headphones off and went and stood in line.

"Hey, how's my favorite human doing today?"

Jupiter felt themselves smiling as they looked up at Rich, the cashier. He was slightly taller than Jupiter, but not by much. His black hair was cut short on the sides with a longer length on top, similar to Jupiter's style. Not that it looked as good on them as it did on Rich. They were pasty from too much time spent indoors, whereas his skin was a silky brown deepened by his time in the skatepark after work. He had a charisma about him that allowed him to interact with everyone. It didn't hurt that when he smiled, his entire face lit up. Most days, he was also the only person that Jupiter talked to.

"I'm doing good. How're you doing?" They hated that their words came out scripted, the same phrase uttered daily.

"I'm doing great. I'm going to go out with some of my buddies after work. They want to take me to this new spot they found. The building just fired its nighttime security officer. It should be awesome."

"Is that legal?" The words left Jupiter's mouth as they thought them.

"Not technically, but don't worry about me. I'll be ok."

He had rung up their items as he spoke. Jupiter handed over their card after checking that the total was the same number as it was the day before and the day before that.

"Have a good lunch, my favorite human."

"Thank you," they said as they grabbed their food and walked outside. Their interaction with Rich always left them lightened, no matter how their morning had gone. The first day when they had picked up lunch, he had misgendered Jupiter. They had responded curtly with their gender and pronouns. Jupiter expected him to get upset, but instead, he just told them, "Oh, all right then," and started calling them his favorite human. They never had to fight to be seen for who they were again, at least during that small period of time.

Outside of the building was a small courtyard full of benches and a few towering palm trees. There was a small group of people that Jupiter didn't recognize, but there were also two of their coworkers. They were part of the marketing team that often worked on the same programs as Jupiter. They were involved in many of the same meetings, and Jupiter smiled at seeing the familiar faces. They walked over to join them but became concerned that that was too forward, so they pivoted at the last minute and sat on the bench on the other side of the sidewalk facing theirs.

The pair looked up briefly and then continued talking. Jupiter put their earphones halfway on their ears, just enough to help with some of the noise but not enough that they couldn't be involved in the conversation.

They took their sandwich and opened the plastic wrap placing it flat on the bench. Then they put their soda on top to hold it down and opened their bag of chips, placing it next to the sandwich. They had set their lunch up the same way since the first day of work, and the familiarity comforted them.

"What a weirdo," one of the two said. Jupiter tried to remember their names. They both started with an A…Ashley or Alison…or maybe it was an H…Heather or Holly. Names were so hard to remember. It didn't help that they both looked alike with their straight hair and slender bodies. Even their clothes were hard to tell apart, except one was dressed in a dark blue shirt while the other wore pink.

"I wonder why they hired her," the blue shirt said.

"Mark said the Austin Tech game specified that one of the developers had to be autistic. Then once she was hired, we were stuck with her even though we've only had one other autistic game," the pink shirt said.

Jupiter remembered the Austin Tech game. It was the first one they had worked on. It was a great action-adventure role-playing game designed to teach math. Jupiter still had the program downloaded on their tablet and would pull it out now and again. The company was great to talk to as well. They constantly interrupted their boss, Mark, and asked for their feedback. And they always used their correct pronouns, unlike their co-workers.

Jupiter picked up the first half of their sandwich and started eating as their co-workers continued to talk.

"I don't know why she had to sit by us. I wish the freak would leave me alone. It is bad enough that I have to sit by her in the office. She smells," the blue shirt said.

"Oh, but remember, Jennifer, we have to call her 'they'. They already complained, and the company fears a lawsuit or something."

"That is so hard. How can they expect me to remember that? But at least I'm glad we don't have to claim it as a woman," Jennifer said.

Jupiter picked up their second sandwich despite not feeling much like eating. Their stomach was tight, and their hands were shaking. They kept their head down, trying not to listen. They wanted to reach up and put their headphones on all the way, but they were afraid it would let them know that they had heard everything said.

The two women began to gather up their lunch items and stood up to leave, but before they did, Jennifer turned and looked directly at Jupiter. They could feel her gaze drill into them even as they avoided eye contact.

"They just need to go somewhere where there are other freaks like them. They need to leave us alone," Jennifer said. Then they walked inside.

Jupiter glanced up and saw people around the courtyard looking directly at them. They found it hard to breathe until they lowered their eyes and focused back on their food.

After their sandwich, they picked up their chips, selecting them one at a time from the bag. As they ate them, they ignored the people and focused on the palm trees nearly as tall as the building itself. Jupiter had been so excited to see palm trees, but now they seemed bare and dull. But Jupiter also envied them a little. They grew tall and swayed into whatever came their way.

After their chips, they picked up their drink, taking their time to finish it, trying to avoid returning to the office as long as possible. Reluctantly, they picked up their trash, threw it away in one of the garbage cans, and walked back inside.

They turned and looked at Rich, busy helping another customer, his smile still on his face. Then they walked into the elevator and pushed the button for lucky number 15. As they returned to their desk, they kept their eyes on the ground, trying to avoid seeing the woman in the blue shirt.

Then they continued playing the game they were testing, the one made for little versions of themselves and thought about all the ways what they did made a difference.

Chapter Three

The next day, they sat at their desk, their hand on their knees to keep them from bouncing up and down. The screen blurred the more they stared at it, and their mouth opened in a deep yawn. They hadn't managed more than four hours of sleep last night after falling asleep with the game controller still in their hand. But they would have still made it to work on time if the bus hadn't been late. They looked around the office one more time, making sure that no one was looking at them. Then they tried to focus back on their screen.

It was the third time they had verified that the correct file was attached to the email. They had triple-checked that they were sending it to their boss and the appropriate people from the marketing team. They read over their message once again. Before they could argue with themselves over if they should write more, they clicked send. The report was done. Weeks of work ready to be scrutinized by the team.

But they had done a thorough job. Their suggestions were sound and evidence-based. Now all they had to do was justify it in their meeting later. An inadvertent groan escaped them, and they looked around to ensure no one had heard before picking up the flashcards on their desk. Then they pulled out their phone and checked the time. Eight minutes.

This isn't a stressful meeting, they reminded themselves. *It's just with your boss. You don't have to present it to the vendor until next week.* It didn't stop the thundering of their heart or the rapid movement of their leg.

They picked up the flashcards and shifted them so fast that it was more for stimulation than reading what was written. They knew what was written on them. Memorizing things that they loved was not hard. It was repeating it back to others when they were staring at you, their eyes trying to drill into your own, while their body language tells you they are judging you even though you can't figure out exactly why. That was the hard part.

A sigh escaped them as they picked their phone back up. Seven minutes.

They had worked hard on the report, documenting areas that could be improved and providing sample language that would work better. They knew this project wasn't like the first one they had worked on. This vendor was more concerned about cost analysis than an ethics review, but they hoped they made their argument well about why improving the content would improve their bottom line.

Jupiter watched the minutes on their phone slowly tick over. They needed to stand up and leave their desk exactly three minutes early. Mark did not like people coming too early to his office for meetings. He also hated when people were late. Three minutes was the ideal time to walk to the other side of the office without arriving too early and having to pace outside his door. He didn't like that either.

At precisely three minutes before the meeting, Jupiter picked up their index cards, holding them in their hands so they were not getting crushed. Then they walked with their head held up towards their boss's office. Despite not being a formal meeting, Jupiter had decided to dress in their suit jacket and pants, the ones they had used for interviews. It gave them the confidence that they needed. However, that confidence disappeared as they saw that their boss's door was not only open; there was someone else sitting in there with him.

They pulled back out their phone and looked at their calendar app, confirming the time and date. They were right. Except doubt flooded through them. A million possibilities flashed through their head almost too fast to process them all, but the most persistent was that this felt like when they would be called down to the principal's office.

"Hi," Jupiter said, stopping at the door.

"Please come and sit down, Ms. Nelly," Mark said.

Jupiter squeezed their hands into fists, crushing the index cards. They had tried correcting him at first, but it had always turned into a lecture on respecting him as a boss. So, they tried to let it go. They tried to tell themselves that it didn't matter that he wouldn't gender them correctly or couldn't learn to pronounce their name. Except that it did matter, maybe it shouldn't, but it did. It mattered a lot.

"Excuse me," they said, trying to speak in the professional tone their grad school advisor had taught them. "My name is Mx. J'naii."

"See, this is what I was talking about." Mark turned and addressed the third person in the room. They were a feminine white person who looked centuries older than Jupiter's thirty years. "Who in their right mind would want to be called mix and mix of what?"

"Yes, I understand," the third person said in a curt tone. "Perhaps I had better handle things from here, Mark." The woman turned to look up at Jupiter. "My name is Nancy, and we wanted to talk with you today. Why don't you take a seat."

The only open seat was the chair next to Nancy and the wall. Jupiter would have to maneuver past their legs and the desk, less than a foot of space. They were not skinny, nor did they have the best balance. It seemed like a recipe for disaster. And then they would be stuck in the spot furthest from the door. But Nancy just scooted their legs to the side slightly, and with a deep breath, Jupiter did their best to inch past without touching the person or the desk. When Jupiter was finally sitting, they turned to the two, expecting them to start the conversation. They just looked at them. Jupiter tried to sort through the conversation in their head and finally found something to say.

"It is nice to meet you, Nancy. May I please ask your pronouns?" Jupiter tried to keep their voice even despite the confusion about the situation. However, as they spoke, Mark's hand came smacking down on his desk, causing them to jump.

"How can she work with our team when she can't even tell someone's gender?" Mark said.

Jupiter was confused at first, trying to figure out who their boss was referencing. Then they realized that he was still not using their correct pronouns.

"I can start by introducing myself. I am Jupiter J'naii, and my pronouns are they and them. They can be confusing if you have not used them before. If so, you can say Jupiter instead." They talked directly to Nancy, hoping Mark would understand that their words were also for him.

"Thank you for introducing yourself to me. I am a woman, and you can address me as such." She spoke slowly, enunciating each word like talking to a small child, not a colleague. Jupiter had been in enough meetings to know this was not a good sign of how things would go.

"Thank you," they said. "This meeting was set up to discuss my report on the Starlight program. Should I start by outlining the points I made in my report?" They took the index cards in both hands and tried to smooth them out as much as possible.

"We will talk about your report to some degree," Nancy said. "However, the agenda of the meeting has changed."

"Oh, I apologize. I did not see an updated meeting agenda come through. Do you have an updated copy?"

Mark sighed loudly and put his hand up to his face. Jupiter tried to figure out what they did to upset him. Sending an updated agenda was considered the correct meeting procedure.

"Mark has asked me to join this meeting because he has concerns over some of your behavior."

Jupiter waited for her to continue, but she stopped talking. This usually meant that Jupiter was supposed to respond, so they repeated Nancy's last statement in their head but could not decide what they were supposed to say. Before they could decide on something, she continued speaking.

"Well, yes, Mark is concerned that working with the last vendor gave you the impression that you don't have to give him proper respect as your manager. He has concerns about how you are constantly correcting him."

"I thought that it was illegal to continually misgender someone in California," Jupiter said, now completely confused. "Discrimination against gender identity is clearly stated on the poster in the lunchroom. The training also said that if the behavior happens once, it may not be considered discrimination. But behavior that happens over a long period, despite being asked otherwise, could be considered discrimination."

"Who the fuck reads the training material?" Mark said.

Nancy looked at him before turning back to Jupiter and continuing. "It is great that you take the training seriously. However, while some of your co-workers may have difficulty with the pronouns that you have chosen to use, you said yourself that they are unfamiliar. You have to be patient while they learn how to use them."

Jupiter wanted to talk about the history of gender-neutral pronouns. They wanted to point out that there was a difference between someone trying and someone continually refusing to use their pronouns. They wanted to scream about how nice and polite they were whenever someone misgendered them. They wanted to let them feel how it felt, like someone was sticking a flagpole in their chest and declaring them to be something they were not. They knew that none of that would help, so instead, they sat in the chair, all their anger and frustration going into their leg, which started to bounce rapidly.

"Yes, your repeated movements are another concern. They are distracting to your coworkers."

"I understand," Jupiter said, their voice coming out calm despite the ocean of emotion that turned inside of them. "When I was hired, I was open about being autistic. I was told that I would be able to work in a sensory-friendly environment. I have expressed my concerns about the cubical I am in. My desk is in the middle of the office, right under a fluorescent light. I previously talked to Mark about this and requested one of the open offices."

"Offices are given based upon seniority," Mark said. "I told you that."

"I understand. It's just that it is very overwhelming. Sometimes, I need to bounce my leg or use one of my fidget devices to help handle the overstimulation. I try to be as non-disruptive as possible. It is not like I am having loud conversations in the middle of the office."

"That is another concern," Nancy said. "You have not acclimated to the other staff. You do not make an effort to fit in with the group. It is becoming disruptive to the team culture."

"They are not very nice," Jupiter said. They started staring at the door as if looking hard enough would allow it to come and swallow them whole, releasing them from this nightmare.

"This is a work environment, not a high school," Nancy said. "We cannot have side groups and cliques. We are one big team here, and we need everyone to ensure they are being team players."

Jupiter closed their eyes then and took a deep breath. They did everything that they could to fit in here. They were so tired at the end of the day that they could barely even manage the mental energy to greet the bus driver. Yet it was not enough. It was never enough.

"It was by no means my intention not to be a team player. I will work on doing better. If you have specific feedback or company training, I would welcome that."

"Well, first, we need to address your report," Mark said. He turned his computer monitor sideways so that everyone could see. Parts of it had been highlighted on the screen, and Jupiter noticed that it was some of their recommendations. They felt more centered like the meeting had finally turned back to something they could speak on.

"Yes, I tried to document my concerns thoroughly. However, I would be happy to clarify anything that I wrote." They grabbed their index cards in two hands and tried to straighten them out again.

"It is your concerns that are the problem," Mark began. "The client did not ask if you thought their game was offensive. You were supposed to be doing bug testing as part of an estimated revenue report."

"No autistic person would want to play a game that says," Jupiter shuffled through their index cards until they found the quote. "'Don't worry that you are unable to understand social skills. We are here to teach you how to communicate correctly.' Also, the game uses the label Asperger's syndrome. That is an out-of-date term in psychological diagnosis and can be found offensive by autistic people. You know, given that it's named after a person that was very harmful to autistic people in World War II."

"Excuse me," Nancy interrupted. "It is always best to use person first language. You should say a person with Asperger's syndrome or a child with Autism."

Jupiter hoped the shock on their face was noticeable, as they could no longer speak. Nancy and Mark had spent the whole meeting being offensive and were now trying to tell them how to talk about Autism. The neurotypical people who wanted to release a derogatory and offensive game were telling them how to speak about being autistic.

"It isn't about the children," Mark said before Jupiter found their own words. "Children with autism will play any game that is put before them. We have to market to the parents. This is what parents want to be taught to their children, and this is what is in the game. You wasted valuable company time on tasks that were not required of you."

And with that, Jupiter found their voice.

"If that is how parents of *autistic children*," Jupiter made sure to emphasize those words, "speak to their children, then maybe what should be created is a video game with sensitivity training for parents and teachers."

"I can't work with this," Mark said. "They do not fit in here. If Austin Industries has any more consulting, we can hire someone else. Keeping them on payroll is a waste."

"This meeting has been most enlightening," Nancy said. "I agree with your report. It is grounds for termination."

Termination. The word echoed around in Jupiter's head until it finally made sense. They were going to get fired.

"I did the bug testing," they said. "I included it all in the report. I was never instructed not to do sensitivity testing, and since it was required on the last project and this one also had a targeted group, I thought it should be included as well."

"No one is questioning your dedication Ms. J'naii," Nancy said.

"It is Mx, Mx. J'naii." The words flow out of Jupiter's mouth harsher than they meant, but the meeting had already drained them.

"We cannot continue to have these outbursts in the workplace. We have written up a severance package. As you have not been employed with us for long, it is only for 30 days of pay, insurance, and a reference for any future employment.

"You're firing me, but will you give me a good reference?"

"Just because you are not a good fit for our company does not mean you will not work better elsewhere. We do not question your dedication and passion."

"You just don't want an autistic nonbinary person working for you."

"Now that is uncalled for," Nancy's voice rose at the offense. "We have extended every courtesy to have you fit into our culture. It did not work out. There is no need to be throwing around baseless accusations."

"You extended every courtesy except using my correct pronouns and prefix. Or how about providing me with a place to work that was not overstimulating? You let your employees say horrid things about me and tell me that I am the one that needs to deal with the situation. It sounds like you needed me for one contract and now don't want to deal with me. If that was the case, you could have just told me so. I would have done the job without getting a lease on an apartment or fully moving to Long Beach."

"Unfortunately, they would not allow us to contract out," Mark said, but he shut his mouth at a glare from Nancy.

"That is enough outbursts," Nancy said. "There are two security officers outside the door. They will escort you to your desk to collect your things. I should not have to tell you that any company property should remain."

Jupiter stood up. Tears were falling down their face, and they felt foolish at being seen so emotional. They were supposed to hold it together and be professional, but they could not keep it inside any longer. As they stood up to walk past, Nancy stopped them.

"You will want to take this." She held up a sealed white envelope.

"What is this?"

"It is your final paycheck and your termination letter." The words were spoken like Jupiter was stupid to have had to ask, like they should know how to react to being fired. As they took the envelope from Nancy's hand, they finally realized that this had been the plan. There was no chance they could have kept their job.

They walked back to their desk with two security officers flanking them. The work in the office had stopped, and Jupiter could feel their eyes drilling into them even though they couldn't see them through the tears.

When they got to their desk, they picked up their bag and looked around for anything they needed to bring home. There was nothing. They didn't even have pictures of a cat telling them to "hang in there" or a printed-off comic. Their space was bare. They looked out over the office seeing everyone else who had made their cubical their own. It was then that they realized that they had never really belonged here. This was never going to be their new home.

Chapter Four

J upiter stood in front of the building, staring down at the check in their hand. It was nearly lunchtime, but they couldn't go back in and order lunch from the small convenience store. Rich had been there watching as the security guards walked them to the front door. It would be too much to have to go back in and explain. Besides, they probably weren't even allowed to go back in.

They would have to deposit the check. They were still using their old bank account from the student credit union, the one they had opened when they had first moved to Illinois. They had been so happy to use their new Illinois ID with their correct gender marker and legally changed name as they opened the account. They had felt like such an adult even though they had already been living on their own for nearly two years after their teacher had accidentally outed them and their parents had kicked them out.

That ID had been special; it was one of the first ones in Illinois to be issued with the non-binary identification. They had to surrender it when they changed to the California ID. But that was fine. California was where they were supposed to start their new life. But they held on to the bank account. They had had that account for over ten years and were reluctant to change it, even though there were no branches in California. They were using direct deposit, and it hadn't seemed like a big deal. Until now, with the rest of their resources in their hand and no way to cash it.

Reluctantly they opened up the envelope and looked at the check. It wasn't enough to last until they found another job. The thought of interviewing again was enough to cause a panic attack. But the security guards were still watching them through the window, and they knew that they needed to move on.

So they started walking, their feet treading the familiar path of the bus route. The bus passed them as they went, but they didn't want to get on and face their empty apartment any earlier than they had to. They didn't want to have to think about how much it cost and how they would not be able to afford it soon. Or about what came next because that would cause a black hole to form inside of themselves, and they knew they would be lost. So they put one foot in front of the other and walked.

Jupiter knew that there were parts of Long Beach that were pretty. There were bike paths and rows of beautiful homes. Some beaches and parks were an oasis in the bustle of city living. But Jupiter only saw that when they ventured out on the weekends. Their part of Long Beach was crowded with buildings next to each other and multiple families living together. There was graffiti on everything and trash all over. People were living out of their cars or on some spot they could claim for their own. Jupiter had always felt for them and had known that the rent was too high for everyone to live. They had known they were lucky to have a job to cover their bills and enough to buy a new video game now and again.

Now though, they knew that they were soon to join them. It just took one bad turn before someone could lose everything. They reached into their pocket, pulled the emergency cash out of their wallet, and walked to the nearest stoplight. They waited for the light to change and walked halfway to where a man held up a sign asking for help and handed over the money before continuing. At least they still had time before it came crashing down on them.

They had made it back to their apartment in three hours. The sun was still high in the sky.

When they entered, they dropped their bag, poured themselves a glass of water, and looked over their space. There was a mattress on the floor, their beanbag, and their pride a joy, a 50-inch tv on top of an entertainment center housing their video game system. It was everything that they owned, but they had worked so hard to get each item to build up their home slowly. Jupiter sat down in the beanbag and stared at the blank tv. They stared for hours, the day's stress having taken everything away from them, leaving them nothing but a shell. Eventually, they drifted off to sleep.

Chapter Five

J upiter woke up as their first alarm went off. They hunted around for their phone, finding it lodged under their leg. The battery showed an angry red, but Jupiter ignored it as they turned off the alarm and tossed the phone on the ground. Then they stood up and started going about their morning routine.

When their second alarm went off, they realized they had nowhere to go. They took their pack of Pop-Tarts and sat back down in their beanbag chair. They broke off tiny pieces eating as slowly as they could. The sugary sweetness turned their stomach, and the dense dough felt like concrete. But they continued to eat, uncertain how else to proceed.

When they finished, they changed out of their day-old clothes and realized it didn't matter what they put on. No one would see. So, they slipped off their binder, crease marks burned into their skin from having it on too long, and threw on some fluffy pajamas. The sleepwear was pink with fairies over them, ugly, but it felt nice. They had been given to them by a roommate in college, and Jupiter had received too few gifts not to treasure the ones they had.

They decided to open the blinds to their window, something they had avoided since moving in. Light poured into their room. Outside their window was a small courtyard that all the apartments faced. Occasionally Jupiter could hear families gathering outside, but most units seemed to keep to themselves. Jupiter preferred their space to be an oasis against the world. But today, Jupiter needed a little connection, so they watched the professionals rush off to work with a pang of jealousy and then the parents corralling their children to school with envy.

Then that, too, was over, and Jupiter was left alone.

They picked up their check from the day before and tried to figure out how to get it cashed. They wished they could pick up the phone and call their parents and ask them what to do, but their parents had made it clear many years ago that they never wanted to speak to them again. That was back when they were a different person. Before they had become Jupiter J'neii, removing any connection to a family that had made it clear they were no longer their child.

Tears started to form in their eyes then. Their chest felt tight, like they could no longer breathe. It happened every time they thought about their family. So they closed their eyes and tried to picture something that made them happy. The trailer to the newest Fantasy Portal game ran through their head, and they felt themselves relax. They allowed the check to fall out of their hands onto a pile of days-old take-out containers. Once the memories had been completely banished, they opened their eyes again and pulled out their laptop.

They loved their laptop, bought it at the start of their second graduate program. Jupiter had gotten it on sale and then spent many nights online gaming with their online friends. But today, they had more mundane things to do.

They pulled up their resume, which they had spent countless hours in the job center working to perfect. There was no one to help them now, so they updated it with their most recent job, hoping that what they put in would work out. They stared at the top of their resume, their pronouns right next to their name. They had thought that if they were honest about who they were, they would find a place to accept them. Apparently, who they were was not good enough.

For the first time in twelve years, they thought about removing their pronouns and going back into the closet. Maybe they could cosplay as a binary gender for eight to ten hours a day. They had known that trans individuals were twice as likely to be unemployed. Somehow they thought they would beat the system. That there was something special enough about them that an employer would take a chance and not regret hiring them. Except one did take a chance, and they did regret it. Now Jupiter was one of the unemployed.

But even if they hid that they were agender, they weren't so sure they could hide that they were autistic. The statistics for autistic people being unemployed were frighteningly high, more than eighty percent, even with a college education. Jupiter had beaten the odds with their last job. An employer looking for someone with autism was statistically unlikely, yet it had happened. And Jupiter had lost it. They had pushed too hard to be accepted for who they were, and now they were back to being alone. Soon they would lose their apartment, the one place they had left. Maybe it was best to give up a part of themselves to keep at least something. If pretending to be cis and neurotypical every day let them pay rent and buy food, then maybe that was enough. But they closed out of the document without removing their pronouns.

Instead, Jupiter opened a web browser and logged into some job sites. They didn't have to stay in Long Beach. There had to be a way out of their lease if they had to move for a job since they couldn't afford it anymore. But even with the geographic space open, there was not much in their field. There was little demand for an educational software consultant, let alone one focused on autism.

After searching through sites endlessly and putting their resume into a few positions they could possibly be qualified for, they finally decided to update their resume on the employment social media platform Connecting. It only took minutes to update their resume and their work status. The finality of clicking the button and letting others know they were looking for work sunk home the reality of their situation.

They were alone. There was no one to go back to. They hadn't seen their parents since they were sixteen. A family had taken them in at that point, but it was only because one of the local parents had taken pity on them. One of the women had been kicked out when she was a teen and convinced her wife to let Jupiter in. Jupiter would always appreciate her, but the women relinquished the connection once the college acceptance letter rolled in.

Jupiter had felt safe at college, their thesis advisor had suggested they were too safe, and when Jupiter had questioned returning for a Ph.D. cautioned them that they needed to go out and explore real life. It took everything, but they left school. They had found a place to be connected and people that would notice if they didn't show up. But now they knew it was all in their head.

Jupiter got up and scrounged through their fridge, pulling out a two-liter of cola. They didn't often drink the hard stuff, as it unsettled their stomach, but they kept a bottle of it in case it was needed, and today it was. They opened the top relaxing at the sound of the carbonation releasing. Then they returned to their chair and, watching the window aimlessly, started drinking their worries away.

Chapter Six

The buzzing sound drilled into their head in synch with the headache.

"Computer, alarm off," they yelled. But for once, their phone refused to respond. They absently swung their hand around their blankets, some part of their brain distantly realizing and being amazed that they had made it to their bed the night before.

Unable to locate their phone, they pulled the pillow on their head, pushing it tightly down. They left just enough space for air but not enough to stop the insistent noise.

Buzz…Buzz…Buzz… They didn't remember their alarm being quite so annoying.

With a groan, Jupiter threw off their covers and toppled out of bed. The sound seemed to echo off the walls, although they knew it had to be their sensory overload because their neighbor was not also pounding on the wall. They shuffled around, hands over their ears to muffle the sound and hold their head together.

Flashes of last night played through their mind. First, it was the emergency 2-liter that had transitioned to the abandoned bottle of vodka. It had been a gift from a work gift exchange and had been left forgotten in their cupboard. They had learned early that alcohol was not a great idea for them. It heightened their already overwhelmed sensory input, but last night they had hoped that maybe one time, it would dampen the loneliness.

Finally, they located their phone. It was plugged into the kitchen counter, where it was supposed to be. They reached for the screen and flicked off the alarm. The silence was instant, along with the relief that allowed the tension to flow out of Jupiter.

Until the phone went off again.

Except, as Jupiter's mind started to wake up, they realized this was not their alarm. It was their ringtone. They couldn't remember the last time someone had called them.

"Stupid telemarketers and scammers," Jupiter muttered as they pushed to end the ringing. They had learned long ago that even the thought of answering a phone call, especially to someone they were not expecting, was enough to trigger a panic attack. Later, when they were mentally prepared, they would check to see if there was a voicemail.

They opened the cupboards to grab some Pop-Tarts and pulled out an empty box. Jupiter hadn't eaten anything else since they were fired, something their pounding head kept reminding them of. So, they rummaged around their kitchen, opening up cupboards they knew were empty but hoping that food would magically appear at some point. It didn't.

Instead, they opened their fridge and found an expired milk carton and some old take-out containers. In the back, they found the remains of an apple, the round form now sunken and brown.

To make things worse, their phone started to ring again. Jupiter flipped off the ringer turning it to vibrate and went to their bathroom. It was a small room with just a toilet, sink, and a stand-up shower, but it served its purpose and was easy to keep clean.

They stared at the shower in distaste, already feeling the water pounding on their skin like thousands of needles. Their naked body on display, a constant reminder of how the world saw them.

Jupiter turned away and looked in the mirror. Their hair was dark brown, cut to the scalp everywhere but the top that wisped up in short peaks. It did nothing to counteract the roundness of their cheeks. Their body was thick and full of curves. Their chest had filled in early and large, causing their peers to tease them with jeal-ousy, grown men admonishing them for trying to tempt them, and an early and deep shame that settled inside them. They tried to restrict their chest with binders, but they were designed for skinny people trying to flatten small mounds. No matter what they did, it looked distorted and wrong, so they hid under baggy clothes.

On the kitchen wall was a Post-it note with the name and number of a doctor. Their job was the first time they had insur-ance to see about medically transitioning. But every time they had thought about calling, panic had seized them. It was like the emotional aftereffects of all the doctor's visits when they were younger.

The first ones had labeled them autistic as a preteen, a label that had given them understanding and identity. Yet, the doctors had talked about them like they weren't even in the room. They didn't like how the doctors told their parents it was ok to mourn for a child they had lost even though they were right there, the same child. They didn't like how they were the first to put a wall between themselves and their parent's love.

But Jupiter was going to do it. They would find someone to talk to about testosterone shots and overcome their anxiety about getting top surgery. Eventually, they were going to become comfortable in their own body. They had just needed more time. And now they had none. Only two more weeks of insurance, not enough time to get seen for an appointment.

They would have to live in their body for longer, so they turned on the water and then turned off the lights. It wasn't completely dark. Light still drifted in from a small window at the top of the shower. It was just enough to allow them to see shadows and nothing more. They quickly undressed and stepped into the stall. The water sliced at them as they did what was needed to be clean and nothing more. Their mind went through the checklist they had been taught the one time they had ended up in the hospital when they were fourteen. Then they shut off the water, took the towel off the towel rack, wrapped it around them, and turned back on the lights.

As they left the bathroom, they heard the phone vibrating on the kitchen counter again. *Someone must have sold their number,* they thought, as they moved to the closet to get dressed.

They pulled out their favorite blue jeans, second binder, and

NASA t-shirt. It was time to face the world, get some food, and make a plan.

Jupiter picked up their phone, surprised when the screen showed it was already noon and they had six missed calls, all from a number they didn't recognize. They knew they would need to block it later, but for now, they jammed the phone in their pocket. Then they searched for their keys dropped somewhere in the haze of the days before.

When Jupiter had first moved to Long Beach, they had been impressed by all the places to get food. There were three fast food restaurants, a diner, and two small grocery stores, all within a ten-minute walk of their house. However, if they wanted a larger store, they had to hop on a bus and transfer once. Since Jupiter knew they had to stop eating out, they decided they had better take the journey to the larger store. They pulled up their phone to look at the bus schedule, and it rang again. Jupiter had almost answered it that time, causing their anxiety to spike and to decide that venturing out in public was not worth it. Then their stomach rumbled, and they trudged to the bus stop. When a text message came through, Jupiter had had enough. They turned off their phone. They would have to wait for the bus without knowing when it would arrive. It was the lesser of the two evils.

It was past one when the bus finally let them off at the grocery store. Their head had not let up the entire ride, and their stomach had joined in with complaining. They relented and went and bought a fast-food burrito before heading into the shop. Then they took their time trying to find the cheapest food. It was nearly four by the time they had made it home with two packed canvas bags, the most they had ever purchased at one time.

They wanted to drop them on the ground and decompress from the hours of being outside in the world, but they knew that if they did not put the groceries away now, they never would. With a sigh, they put the bags on the counter and moved the contents unceremoniously into the cupboards. By the time they were finished, Jupiter was exhausted; all they could do was plop down into their beanbag chair. Their phone cut into them as they sat, so they reached back and pulled it out.

Reluctantly they decided to turn their phone back on. Jupiter loved their phone. It played games and allowed them to connect to forums and social media. It was their outlet for friendship that allowed them to interact when they had the mental ability to do so. However, the minute it reminded them it was actually a phone with voice calls and text messages, it became an item they despised. They had just never been able to handle people contacting them without notice. The only thing worse than a phone call was an unexpected knock on the door.

And sure enough, as soon as their phone loaded, messages began to fill up their notifications. There were another six missed calls and two text messages, all from the same number. Jupiter dropped their phone on the ground like it could poison them, then started their video game system. They needed a really good gaming session to drive away their troubles. Then tomorrow, they could pick up the pieces of their life. Or at least try.

But as they loaded the game, their mind wandered to the little red notification symbol on their phone. They couldn't see it. The screen wasn't even turned on, but still, it drilled into their brain, calling attention to itself.

"I can just read the text," Jupiter muttered to themselves.

They picked up the phone and selected their messages before losing the nerve.

> Mx. J'neii, I am consulting you to let you know that we have a position available as an educational consultant for Austin School District. Our founder is very interested in recruiting you and would like to offer you an interview as soon as possible.

That has to be spam, they thought, *even if they did gender me correctly.* Then they continued to the next message.

> I assure you that this is a legit position. We were disheartened to hear about your terminated contract and wish to bring you into our employ full-time. Please get in touch with me at your earliest convenience.

> However, today would be preferred.

The thought that someone would want to recruit them was faltering, but they also knew that is how spammers get you, the appeal to your emotions. They had learned the hard way too often and would not fall for it now.

Yet, something about the message seemed familiar to them. Then they realized that it was Austin School District. In their first project, they worked for Austin Industries. Jupiter had thought that it was weird to be contracted to one of the biggest technology companies, the one with technology like hyper-realistic virtual headsets, augmented reality glasses, and even their new virtual tablet, that worked as a hub allowing interactions to be virtually hands-free. Jupiter had spent hours watching reviews on the internet, but all of it was out of their price range.

However, none of that connected to why they would want to release a game specifically for autistic kids. So, Jupiter did what they did best and went and scoured the internet for an answer. They found it in a profile piece about Austin Pierce, the 30-year-old billionaire who had confirmed that he was autistic and made mention of the difficult time that he had at school. It was why he had decided to create a nonprofit school system specifically for autistic and other neurodivergent children. The school system wasn't named, but Jupiter would swear that it would be called Austin School District. He named everything after himself, and Jupiter couldn't help wondering if he was incredibly narcissistic or just awful at naming things.

The game had been abandoned on the title screen, and with new concerns about electricity bills, Jupiter turned it off and focused on their laptop. They pulled up a web browser, but before they could open up a new tab, their screen began to buzz. Connect was still open, and there was a message from someone named Stanley Thompson that said precisely what was in the text messages.

Jupiter ignored his message and clicked on his name instead.

His profile pulled up a picture that almost looked like a realistic VR avatar. His job title was listed as Superintendent for Austin School District. *Superintendent,* Jupiter thought, *that sounds too important to be doing simple recruiting.*

They clicked on Austin School District, and it pulled up a company page. The site was basic, embarrassingly so if it was supposed to be connected to a tech company. There was only a stock photo of a school building and a generic-sounding mission statement. "Austin School District was founded by Austin Pierce to help autistic and neurodivergent children to learn in an environment that is built around their needs."

Then there was an email address.

The website dinged again, letting them know they had a new message.

> I understand that this is not typically how job applications go. I apologize for calling your phone. It is only that Mr. Austin is very concerned about recruiting you. I think he feels slightly responsible for how you were treated.

Jupiter stared at the message, and before they knew it, Jupiter responded.

> Why would he feel responsible?

> ASPEX presented itself as an ally. They had a strong history of working on games with autistic clientele. As you probably know, not many educational technology companies specialize in that market. However, Mr. Austin always prefers to work with teams that have at least one autistic team member, especially if the project is for autistic individuals. Hiring you was a condition of the contract. He didn't realize how they would treat you. Now he feels it is best to hire you directly. He will no longer be working with ASPEX and will advise others against it as well.

Jupiter stared at the message reading it, and then read it again. It seemed incomplete, so finally, they asked.

How does he know how they treated me?

Then, after a short pause, Jupiter's brain caught up with everything they read. They texted again.

Wait, he recommended me personally?

Jupiter waited as the typing icon flashed. Their fingers began tapping on the side of their touchpad, a habit they had formed in college. The three dots took up their entire field of vision as they tried to remember to breathe. Finally, the response appeared.

Yes, he recommended you personally. He saw you present at a conference and was impressed with your work. However, he did not make them hire you. That was ultimately their choice. He knows you were fired because one of his project managers called about a new contract. The picture that ASPEX tried to convey about you was not pleasant. Unfortunately, it is a behavior we have seen before. We understand better than most how much ablism there is in the workforce.

Jupiter sat back, their eyes taking in the message several times before the words started connecting with their brain. Once they realized what was being said, a mix of emotions flooded through them. There was anger at ASPEX for trying to justify firing them after all the hurtful things they said. There was a validation at being recognized for how hard it was to be seen as capable just because they were autistic. They processed the emotions logically, thinking through each one and filing it away. But there was one thing missing from the message.

> It wasn't just the autism. I'm nonbinary, and they wouldn't use my correct pronouns.

The reply was instantaneous.

> That wouldn't happen here. I'm sure you know that many people who are autistic are also less likely to adhere to gender norms. There are many students and staff who are nonbinary and trans.

Jupiter tried to remember the last time they were around other trans people. There were a few pride events, but the noise was so much they had stopped trying to attend. There was one student in high school, the one that had first handed them a book that gave them the language they needed. But they hadn't hung out, and he graduated a few months later. Jupiter was sure there were more trans students in college, but it wasn't the safest place to be out, and Jupiter was not very good at meeting other people.

> Are you serious that this is real?

They knew it was a stupid thing to type even as they typed it. Yet, they still had to ask to get some verification to have it all make sense to them.

> It is real. You will have an interview tomorrow. Tomorrow morning you will receive a package. I've already shipped it out. When it arrives, open it and join me for your interview. Don't worry about being late. The directions will be stored in the device. Follow them, and you will be fine. If you run into any problems, then you can text me. However, think hard before you do. That will be considered a forfeit of your interview, and you will be denied the position. I look forward to meeting you tomorrow.

Then immediately, Stanley's status switched from available to offline. Jupiter sat looking at the message, trying to understand what it meant. It went so well until then, but they were back to wondering if any of it was real.

A text message came through on their phone from the same number. It was a tracking number. Jupiter clicked on it and saw that a delivery was expected to be made before ten a.m. the next day.

It wasn't until later, after Jupiter had logged in to escape into their games, that they thought to question how exactly Stanley had gotten their address.

Chapter Seven

Jupiter picked up their phone from where it laid on the bed next to them. The screen flared to life, showing the time: 4:32. With a sigh, they dropped it back on the bed and turned over to stare at the dark ceiling.

So much for trying to go to bed early, they thought.

They took deep breaths, trying to relax the tension out of their muscles. It just cleared their mind for thoughts to flitter. *Was it even real? What if they don't like me? What was it all about anyway? Who is this company, and why would they want someone to hire me? I wasn't even good at that presentation. I was so scared I could barely breathe, and after finishing, I went to my hotel room and dry-heaved for the rest of the afternoon. Then I sat on the bed and watched old movies for the rest of the night.*

The thoughts raced through their head, each coming before the last thought finished. They tried to push the ideas away and focus on something different. Their current before-bed mind movie was based on their favorite childhood role-playing game. A young man from a small village had to journey to save a princess captured by dark magic. Except in Jupiter's version, they had rewritten it, so the main character was a trans man forced out by his village. The princess was who everyone expected him to be, and he had locked her up far away. Now he was journeying in the world, not to save it, but to find his way in it as his true self.

The main character, Blade, had just entered a racing competition that used dinosaur-like creatures as mounts. Jupiter had gone to sleep before the race had happened, and they fell back into the world, watching the story in pictures flashing through their mind.

Until a loud pounding noise startled them awake, causing them to fall out of bed, the sheets still wrapped around their body. They looked around, trying to find a hiding place, before they realized sunlight was sneaking under the blinds and someone was knocking at their door.

When the second knock came, they reached up with one arm feeling around until they found their phone. It was 10:28 in the morning. They stood up and picked up the sheet, wrapping it around their body as they walked to the door. They opened it just enough to peek their face through, but it was enough for the sun to assault them, and they recoiled, closing their eyes until they could adjust to the brightness. When they opened them again, they saw a woman in a brown shirt and shorts staring at them with a tight jaw and bunched eyebrows.

They are annoyed, Jupiter thought proud of themselves for recognizing the gesture so early in the morning. *Oh, they are annoyed.* The thought caught up with them.

"Sorry," they said as they noticed the woman holding a tablet for Jupiter's signature. Jupiter took it from her and signed their name, then the woman handed them a brown box, about a foot cubed in size.

"Thank you," Jupiter managed, but the woman was already walking through the front gate back to her truck.

Jupiter eyed the box as they closed the door. They checked the mailing label and saw that the return address said Austin Technology, but they couldn't imagine what was in the box that would allow them to do an interview. *It could be a phone*, Jupiter thought, *but they already have my number.*

They wanted to tear into the packaging and find out what was inside, but they were still dressed in a t-shirt and boxers, and it wouldn't do to attend a job interview like that, even one held virtually. So, they placed the box on their kitchen counter and dressed in their nicest collared shirt and only suit jacket. They thought about wearing sweats. After all, it was a virtual meeting. But their uncertainty would not allow them to settle for anything less than their suit pants, just in case.

Once they were dressed, they picked up the box and took it to their beanbag chair. It was secured with Jupiter's favorite type of tape. It was the paper type that was stuck but made it easy to open without having to find something sharp. They made quick work of the box but stood frozen upon seeing the contents.

It was an Austin Technology VR345 headset.

They sat looking at the solid black box with the Austin Technology logo, a silver globe of the earth with a cursive AT cut out of the middle. Then there in silver lettering was the VR345 headset.

There were no pictures. There was nothing else to indicate what this product would be because it wasn't supposed to exist.

It was an urban legend of the internet.

Sure, some streamers obtained what they claimed was an AT VR345. They came packaged in the same solid black box with silver lettering. But when they took the product out of the box, it never worked.

The current theory was that you had to have a password to activate the technology. If you could get one to work, it is supposed to be the ultimate virtual reality simulation, one indistinguishable from real life. The avatars had full body and facial movement without any tracking technology built into the headset.

Jupiter had once watched an unboxing from a streamer that had paid more than $50,000 to open it up and found that it did nothing. The streamer had kept it as a prop in the background of videos for a month before it disappeared. The streamer refused to speak about it ever again.

And Jupiter had one sitting in their living room.

Gently they took it out of the packing box. The black box was solid on all sides except the bottom, where it was taped with those easy-to-pull plastic tabs. Completely sealed, Jupiter was sure they could sell this for enough to not have to worry about working for at least another year. Once they opened it, the value would decrease exponentially.

They let the weight of it settle in their hands as they admired the glossy finish of the box. Finally, they put it gently on the carpet in front of them. They picked up the packing box and flipped it to the side when a small slip of paper fell out. Jupiter picked it up and saw that it was a packing slip with the shipping information. It also had a typed note.

This is your interview. Turn it on and meet me, and the job
is yours. I have faith that you can do it.

    - Stanley Thompson

Sighing, they set the note on the ground and turned over the black box. As they ripped open the tabs, they felt a tear fall down their cheek. With that done, they knew they had to do whatever it took to get this job, even though they still had no idea what the job was.

The top of the box slid off easily. The first thing Jupiter saw was a cardboard topping with writing on the top. They took it out and looked at it.

"Only authorized persons are allowed to be in possession of the AT AS VR345. If you are not authorized, you are in violation and will be prosecuted for harboring stolen technology. You may contact us using the information below to remit the technology with little to no repercussions." An email and phone number followed the writing. Then there was a lengthy legal statement in small print. This had never been shown on any stream. No one probably wanted to admit on camera that they knew their actions were illegal. But it was also an unusual statement on a piece of technology.

Part of Jupiter wanted to box up the headset and send it back with an apology note. However, they were meant to have this. They reached down to the letter and read it through one more time. Somehow this headset was connected to their job interview. They just had to get it to work.

Jupiter closed their eyes and took a deep breath before returning to the box.

Inside there were two smaller boxes that fit next to each other, long and slim. They were the same glossy black box material. Both boxes with the silver Austin Technology logo. One box was labeled AT AS AG345 in crisp silver lettering. The second box was labeled AT AS VR345. Jupiter could never remember the headset being referred to with the AS labeling, even though the boxes they remembered were similar to the ones they now had.

They pulled the AG345 box out and carefully slid off the lid. Inside was an unassuming pair of black-framed glasses in a molded foam platform. Jupiter picked them up, surprised by how light they were. They opened the arms and noticed the inside was studded with slightly raised silver buttons. Jupiter ran their fingers over them, but they felt solid and immovable. It was such an interesting choice that Jupiter knew they must have a function.

In the few videos they had watched, this was as far as things had gone. The glasses turned on, and the steamers reported seeing a giant red X across their field of vision. Then the glasses flashed a warning sign and shut down.

As Jupiter let go of the start button, they saw a classic loading bar appear. It was a short time before that was replaced with the tech circle of death. The next step was the red X, except they didn't see that. Instead, the word "evaluating" appeared. Then it disappeared and was replaced by a new message, "Start neural scan."

No video had talked about this. Jupiter examined the box and noticed a circle in the middle of the foam packaging. They reached down and pulled. The foam came out easily, and underneath there was a thin cardboard white sleeve held together by two white tabs. Jupiter opened it up and pulled out what looked like a plastic cap with more silver metal studs. They unfolded it to find an EEG cap. On the side was a row of indented silver clasps that matched perfectly with the buttons on the arm of the glasses.

Once the cap was open, it was easy to see how to put it on their head. The part for the back was larger and rounded. Jupiter slipped it on, and it fit easily over their shorter hair. Then they moved the arms of the glasses to line up. Instantly the glasses responded with a cartoon-style brain that jumped up and down.

"We are now scanning your brain," the audio was unexpected as Jupiter did not notice any speakers in the glasses, but it was clear, like the brain was talking right next to them. Below the brain, the words appeared in closed captioning.

"We need to get to know what makes you, you," the brain continued in an androgynous voice. "We are going to show you some images and videos. At times there will be music or talking. To better understand how your brain works, some things may be sad or make you a little angry. You can choose to stop testing now, but you will be unable to continue. We wouldn't do this if it weren't needed. And you do not have to worry; there will be no sad animal pictures. We would never do that to you. If we show anything too distressing or play anything that causes harm, we should be able to tell pretty fast, even the first time, and we will change stimuli as soon as possible. The process will take between thirty minutes to two hours. So enjoy." The brain gained a top hat and a cane and danced off the side of the glasses.

The images started gently with summer days full of wildflowers, and Jupiter's mind wandered back to the introduction. It was almost written like it was meant to address people with autism specifically. *AS - Autism Spectrum. Did they label the headset for autistic people? That couldn't be it, could it?* But before Jupiter could think more about it, the images changed, grabbing their attention.

They were so transfixed that Jupiter didn't realize when the images had finally stopped and the word "Congratulations" flashed across their room. The display was no longer 2D. Instead, the words had substance, like they were as substantial as the TV.

Then the words disappeared, and instructions took their place.

"It is now time to enter AVR. Please remove the neural cap and put on the virtual reality cover and interactive gloves." It was the same voice as the brain, and Jupiter found they missed the little cartoon creature. But they dutifully removed the plastic cap and opened the second box.

At the top were gloves that Jupiter slipped on. They were made out of thin, flexible material. Looking at them, Jupiter could not see how there was any technology in them, let alone how they would be used for movement.

Inside was a covering, almost like a case for the glasses. Using the images that Jupiter now saw projected in their living room, they slid the thin, rigid sleeve over the AR glasses. With the covering secure, they could no longer see, except light escaping in from the sides and a flattened graphic of the directions. Jupiter felt for the thick cloth that enclosed the VR case. The top material connected directly to the forehead with what looked like a sticky tap with a silver button. The side cloth had another sticky tap that connected above the ear, with the bottom directly connecting to the glasses' arm. The base was a firm plastic that blocked out light by sealing it against the cheeks.

When everything was attached, the directions disappeared, and letters began to appear. They were written in the pixelated font of the first video games, and when Jupiter read them, a chill ran down their spine.

"Welcome to Autism Virtual Reality. Enjoy."

Chapter Eight

The lettering broke apart into specks of light and floated up into the sky until Jupiter stood in darkness. They waited for something else to appear. When nothing did, they turned their head around, peering into the void, hoping this wasn't some elaborate hoax. They wanted this to be real so bad that it burned inside them.

SETUP MODE

The words appeared in front of them in simple white text. As soon as Jupiter finished reading them, they disappeared, replaced by new text.

DO YOU USE A WHEELCHAIR OR OTHER MOBILITY DEVICE?

No, Jupiter thought as they read the words. But before they could figure out how to answer, the text disappeared again.

YOU ARE STANDING.

Jupiter had thought of themselves as standing as soon as they had entered the world. It wasn't until the words appeared that they realized their perception differed from what was happening outside the headset. There they were sitting on their beanbag chair with nice clothes that caused their skin to itch and their binder pressing tightly against their chest. Then they were back in the black void where they felt like they were standing, and their physical body was distant again. The words drifted away, almost as if they were waiting for Jupiter to finish their internal monologue.

FOLLOW THE WHITE SPOT.

A large white spot appeared about six feet in front of them. A bright yellow arrow appeared, starting at Jupiter's perception of where their feet would be and then stretching until it reached the spot.

It was apparent that it was trying to tell them to move, but they knew that already. What it did not tell them was how to move.

They tried waving their hands around, flailing them in front of the headset like that would make a hidden menu appear. Then they tried to touch their fingers together and then their palms. Nothing happened.

Then their thoughts started to spiral. *Why could I make this work when so many others couldn't? It probably isn't real, just a basic program, a cruel practical joke designed to trick me. I will never get to my interview if I can't figure out how to move six feet in a virtual space. I'm a horrible gamer. I don't even deserve to be called a gamer.*

IT'S OK. YOU ARE DOING OK. JUST WALK.

At some point during their spike of anxiety, the text had changed. They let the positive words settle them and then took a few deep breaths to reorient themselves.

You know what I'm thinking, Jupiter thought. *If you can respond to my anxiety, you may respond to other thoughts.*

Jupiter looked at the white spot and walked over to it. If someone were to ask Jupiter what they did, they wouldn't have been able to explain any more than they could have explained how they walked with their physical body. They just knew they could do it and then did it.

WELL DONE.

Jupiter felt a glow inside of them when reading the words. They had so little praise growing up, and even as an adult, they thought they would do almost anything to hear someone say nice things. They knew it was why they enjoyed video games so much. You completed a set quest, and then some NPC, a non-playable character, told them how well they had done.

The words disappeared again.

CONGRATULATIONS. YOU HAVE FINISHED THE TRAINING.

One last thing to do.
Follow the yellow road.

The world fell back into complete darkness before a pale-yellow shape appeared at their feet and then spread out, curving into the blackness.

Jupiter looked down at the road. It was a dull pastel yellow with no variation. *The least it can have is some lines running down the middle,* Jupiter thought. *Maybe you could turn it into a proper yellow brick road. Then I can be like Dorothy, off to visit Oz.*

At the thought, the road turned a brighter gold and filled in with a brick pattern. The area under their virtual feet became harder and slightly uneven. Bright green grass sprouted off on each side, off the road. It looked so real that Jupiter reached down and felt the coarseness of the blades slide across their palms.

It wasn't quite right. There was something muted about each of the feelings, but it was a virtual world, and they shouldn't have been able to feel anything at all.

And the smell. There was just a hint of the scent of grass and springtime. It was almost like it had been built from their memory.

They took a moment to appreciate the world. Then they turned their focus back on what they needed to do. At the end of this road was a job interview, one that was hopefully connected in some way to this virtual world. Now they just had to get to it. So they started walking.

As they walked, they looked around, but there still was not much to see. The grass stretched off to the sides, and the road continued forward. It didn't take long before even the novelty of the virtual program wore off.

It would be nice if there were something else to look at while I walk, they thought. As if summoned, a tree appeared ahead of them. It was large, with thick branches that started close to the ground, making climbing easy. It had been Jupiter's favorite type of tree as a kid. They had taken their pocket games and stayed in the branches for hours.

They continued until the tree was lost behind them. Then a picnic area appeared. It was a perfect setup, like the kind Jupiter saw in movies and longed to visit with a family of their own. The bench was light brown and clean. There were no names carved on its surface, no food littered around, not even a train of ants. Next to it was a public barbecue that looked like it had never been used. It was the perfect thing to appear on this spring day, and Jupiter knew that is why it was here.

It was an amazing program. Jupiter was wholly immersed, unlike any virtual reality machine they had ever tried. The program was amazing. It was almost like they were here and not sitting in their living room. Visually everything was perfect, in an impossible way. It was the rest of their senses that were muted, reminding them that it wasn't real. But it was still the best video game experience they had ever had if it weren't so boring.

What this needs is some conflict, Jupiter thought. *There needs to be something to work towards to give the user a dose of dopamine and keep them engaged.*

The world went dark, the contrast between the bright spring day was jarring, and Jupiter felt their palms sweat and their fingers tense. But just as fast, the world changed again, as if the darkness was just a reset.

The road was now gone, and in its place was a soft mat full of red and blue foam tiles. They covered an area about the size of a school gymnasium. More words appeared above them in the sky.

SURVIVE

Then the words disappeared, and a new menu floated in the sky. It looked like a scroll, an animated one that you may find in a fantasy game. At the top, it was labeled "tasks" in bold calligraphic text. Below that, there was just one item … survive.

A timer appeared next to the scroll. It stood frozen at five minutes, and then the digits started counting down … 4:59 … 4:58 … 4:57 …

Jupiter looked around to try and figure out who they were supposed to fight, but there was nothing there.

Well, this is boring, they thought. As if in response, a thunderous roar filled the arena. The sound caused Jupiter to freeze, not in fear but in delight. They were so often overwhelmed by noises, yet this one was at a perfect pitch and volume, enough that they knew to pay attention but not enough that they threw their hands to their ears to help protect them from the sound.

They were so caught up in the noise that they almost missed the shadow that passed over them. It wasn't until the second bellow that they remembered where they were and saw the dragon. It was such a beautiful dragon. It was so large that if it landed, it would have taken up at least half of the playing field. The top of the body was filled with green scales that shimmered with a rainbow glow. They were detailed enough that even from a distance, Jupiter could see the textured lines on each one and the slight shadow of where they overlapped. The underside looked like thick leather, a softer green than the scales. The wings were spread out fully and looked webbed like a bat but in the same deep green color. And there were four legs, the back ones larger with long black claws that were headed straight for them.

All at once Jupiter remembered that they were in a game, and while some distant part of their brain was fairly certain that this dragon could not harm them, the rest of them felt like it was not worth the chance. As the dragon swooped towards them, they dropped and raised their hands to cover their face.

It was a pathetic, cowardly move, but it seemed to be enough for the dragon to pass them by and head back up to the sky. Jupiter watched as it lapped around the arena and flinched back as it let out a large stream of fire.

Oh shit, they thought. It all felt so real, and they didn't know what to do. Then they saw the task - survive. They just had to survive. The time had continued counting down … 3:46 … 3:45 … 3:44 … They looked around for a weapon stand, some mythical sword that would allow them to defeat the beast. There was nothing but the mat, the scroll, and the timer.

Survive.

At once, Jupiter realized they were not supposed to win some epic battle. This was a mini-quest, one designed to teach them how to maneuver better. The next time the dragon swooped down, they launched into a double front roll, returning to a standing position. The dragon came back, and this time Jupiter sprinted fast, like a speedster. One second, they were at one side of the mat, and the next, they were on the other side, running into an invisible barrier that caused them to fall back on their invisible butt.

They got up quickly, ready for the dragon this time, but the timer finished the last of its countdown and flashed 00:00. On the task scroll, a line crossed through survive. They had accomplished their goal.

The mat disappeared, replaced by the yellow brick road again. Jupiter stepped onto it with excitement. They started running so fast that the blades of grass were a blurry streak on either side of them. It felt perfectly natural, not even a suggestion of motion sickness. An excitement bubbled up inside of them. In this world, they were capable of everything.

So they ran.

They kept running.

Then the excitement began to wear off. What was the point of running fast if there was nowhere to go?

They knew there was a challenge, something they were not figuring out. This was a trial, a way to prove that they were worthy of the position. They had finished the first trial, the first round. There had to be another challenge. They just had to find it.

The world disappeared again, leaving Jupiter in darkness. This time they welcomed it. They knew what came next.

Bright white letters filled up the sky.

Round Two

Underneath the words, a portal appeared. It was a metallic blue hole in reality, and Jupiter knew what was expected of them. They stepped through.

Chapter Nine

They entered a room with speckled blue tiles on the floor and white-painted concrete walls. The space was filled with desks with wooden writing tops, just big enough for a book and notebook. It was stretched over a metal frame on one side until it reached an orange hard plastic chair. The desks were scattered over the classroom, spaced far enough that it was easy to walk between them.

Jupiter went to line the desks up in the neat rows they remembered from school when they stopped and looked at the room again. There was a pattern here, if a disorganized one. The desks appeared to be grouped into four clusters. The task scroll appeared as soon as the thought popped into Jupiter's head. This time it was attached to one of the blank walls. A new task was written on it under the completed assignment: Enter the portals and observe.

Four portals appeared, one around each cluster of desks. They were long and oval-shaped, perfect for a person to step through the swirl of blue.

There was nothing to distinguish the portals from each other, so Jupiter headed towards one at random and stepped through.

One second, they were in the classroom, and the next, they were in outer space surrounded by darkness except for the Earth hovering in front of them, the glow of the sun's rays bouncing off the atmosphere.

If Jupiter had a mouth at that moment, they knew it would have been hanging open, their eyes wide as they gazed, unmoving. It wasn't just the transition from one place to another, although that was dramatic enough; it was where they had ended up.

As a kid, they had pored over astronomy books, admiring the beauty of the solar system, hoping one day to escape from their small town, escape the entire planet. It was why they had named themselves Jupiter, the most beautiful of all Sol's planets, with a storm twice as large as Earth that had been blazing for more than a century. That passion resonated with them.

Now they were here, with nothing separating them from the emptiness of space. Somewhere in their head, they knew this was all a simulation, but it didn't stop it from feeling so real.

Then Jupiter heard a soft hum, like someone was quietly murmuring without stopping in between words. Next to them was a lanky preteen, or the avatar of one. Jupiter tore their attention away from the planet and looked at the child. A nameplate appeared, "Aaron (he/him)," then disappeared once Jupiter finished reading it. The boy had short brown hair, light skin, and a patch of freckles across his checks. He wore jeans and a black t-shirt with "Roll for Initiative" in white lettering, and no shoes.

Jupiter liked the kid instantly. As he talked, his voice was muted, but his lips were moving, showing off braces on his teeth. The detail was intricate, each bracket lined up perfectly with each tooth, and there was no lag as his lips moved.

The boy was looking down at Earth as he muttered. Occasionally, he would gesture with his hand and turn the Earth around to look at a different continent. Then suddenly, the Earth began to glow. Boundaries became drawn in neon colors and capitals and important monuments were labeled.

Jupiter watched as Aaron seemed to focus on Europe. The boy's fingers moved as if typing on a virtual keyboard, and the world below reshaped itself. The globe was gone, and in its place, Europe floating in space. On the continent were avatars of soldiers, the uniforms all different, matching up to their countries. As the boy spoke, the avatars would move. Sometimes the boy would gesture, bringing up clips of actual war footage.

He was processing the events, going back over moments that were needed. When he asked what Jupiter assumed were questions, the world responded. Jupiter didn't know what they were more amazed by, that the program understood what he was saying with what appeared to be amazing accuracy, or how it allowed for learning of not only events but critical thinking.

This is what school should be, Jupiter thought. And just as suddenly as they had landed in space, they found themselves back in the classroom.

The change in scenery was disconcerting. Yet the more they thought about what they had seen, the more they became excited for what waited on the other side of the next portal.

Chapter Ten

Jupiter was prepared for the sudden shift in perception this time. Or they thought that they were. However, the world they entered was bright, and it was all they could initially register as the color overloaded them. They closed their eyes, allowing their brain to rest before they opened them up again. The overwhelming brightness was still there, but a filter seemed to be thrown over the world, toning it down to a level that Jupiter could manage. It was almost like the motion sickness filters in older VR models, which turned the edges of the field of vision black, causing tunnel vision.

There was still color everywhere. The grass was bright neon green. The trees had neon purple trunks and hot pink leaves. There were fields of neon flowers of all colors. It was Jupiter's idea of a nightmare, but the child in the middle of a grass field seemed very happy. *El (e/em)*, eir nameplate flashed above eir head, then disappeared.

El was young, maybe six or seven years of age. E wore a blue beanie that hid all eir hair and had on a t-shirt with a rainbow unicorn doing a dab and some blue sweatpants. The right hand of eir avatar was in front of eir virtual face, eir fingers flicking rapidly in front of eir eye. El had a big, bright smile. E was sitting in the grass, bouncing up and down, eir eyes darting around.

The world that e was in was like a giant storybook. In front of the child, propped on a purple tree stump, was a picture book. The pages automatically turned as needed. The words were also projected in the air above El, similar to what Jupiter had seen before. A narrator was reading as the world moved around em, like the pictures from the book, except it had all been remade in 3-D and dipped in neon paint.

Every so often, the narrator would stop and ask El a question. The first time, one of the words, "rabbit," moved out of the story and focused in front of the child. "What does this word say?" the narrator asked. However, instead of expecting the child to speak, a rabbit, a frog, and a dog all stepped in front of the child. The child reached down and picked up the rabbit, holding it in eir arms as the story continued.

Next, the word "jump" broke off from the text, and the narrator asked the child to do what the word said. The child squealed in delight as e stood up and jumped, the rabbit still firmly in eir arms.

The story continued, pausing every so often to ask the child questions. The question types changed, but no matter what was asked, the child answered straight away, even typing in the spelling of simple words. Without being expected to speak, the child demonstrated their ability to read. It was a genuinely interactive and independent learning environment.

But as El reached the end of the story, the narrator did ask the young student to read. It was just a short passage full of the words that the child had already demonstrated that eir knew. Jupiter waited for frustration from the child. Instead, there was silence. The words slowly highlighted as the child focused on them. Then, the narrator came on with a proud voice congratulating em for finishing the passage. The child jumped up and down, then kissed the bunny on its head and disappeared.

Jupiter found themselves back in the classroom. The white walls suddenly seemed dim in comparison to the magical forest. They knew they needed to enter another portal, but they couldn't, not yet. Their mind was still reeling from what they had seen.

Jupiter had built a reading program for their master's thesis. It was designed for nonverbal individuals to be able to interact by pushing buttons on a tablet. The idea seemed so simple compared to what they had just seen. For the first time, they realized the possibilities in front of them. Completely immersive and interactive curriculum set in a virtual world. To be able to provide that to autistic children would be amazing.

But not once had anyone mentioned that anything like this was possible, let alone already in development. Children were here, learning in these programs. Somewhere, someone wanted them to be a part of it. Jupiter sat down at one of the desks, overwhelmed. They tried to breathe, allowing their brain to process everything they had seen until they reached one crucial conclusion. This wasn't just about being able to interact with cool tech;

this was finally a way to change the entire educational experience for autistic children. They wanted to be a part of that. They needed to be a part of it. So, they stood up and walked toward the third portal.

Chapter Eleven

They eagerly stepped into the third portal, unsure of what they would find. It opened up in a neighborhood lined with identical houses up and down the street. The lawns were unnaturally bright green with a perfect cut. A sun hung in the air, showing the day to be midmorning. It would be the picture of a perfect utopia if it were not so unnatural. The brightness of the day did not match up with the air-conditioned chill that Jupiter felt. But it was more than that. The world looked empty, missing all the families occupying the space. There were no toys left out in yards or cars in driveways.

A loud buzzing noise cut through the scene, causing Jupiter to tense at the noise before the program adjusted to something that could be handled. The buzzing continued incessantly, causing Jupiter to turn around to look for its source.

Behind them was the skeletal frame of one of the idyllic manors. It looked out of place, like a crime scene in the middle of paradise. Except, as Jupiter looked closer, they saw not death but slow growth. The house was framed with light brown wood and held up by a foundation of more wood. Some of the walls had started to be filled in, but most were open.

The only person in sight was a teenager wearing overalls concentrating on a power saw that was the source of the annoyance. Jupiter walked closer to them. *Tiffany (she/her).* The nameplate seemed so natural now that Jupiter registered it just enough to pick up the information before it disappeared. Tiffany wore plastic safety glasses over her eyes, thick ear coverings, and a face mask. Her hands were covered in thick gloves. On her head was one of those yellow plastic hard hats, and Jupiter was not surprised to look down and see work boots covering her feet. Even in the virtual environment, she used all the proper protective gear.

Jupiter stood back and watched, amazed at what she saw. Tiffany was handling the power saw like she knew exactly what she was doing. She was cutting a two-by-four, her hands gliding the wood along the sharp blade. Her mind was focused like nothing else mattered except what was happening before her.

The saw stopped, and Tiffany moved the wood over a collection of cut pieces. She began assembling them, lining up each piece and hammering them with a precision that left Jupiter in awe.

That, more than anything, made Jupiter realize that this simulation was a version of technical training. Tiffany was learning to build a house in a safe environment. These were fundamental skills that she would have to take toward employment.

But how much like real life is it, Jupiter thought as they walked to the equipment, feeling the cool metal frame with their hands.

Jupiter was grateful when the hammering finally stopped. They knew they were here to learn, but even muted, the sounds were becoming unbearable. So they turned and focused, hoping to be able to leave fast.

Tiffany's hands were moving. At first, Jupiter thought she was stimming, moving her hands in a sensory-seeking way, but there must have been some personal input panel because they were no longer alone. A six-foot-tall masculine NPC emerged next to the girl. He towered over her, but it was obvious who was in charge as she pointed and made gestures with her hands. Together, they lifted the built structure, a new wall frame, and carried it towards the house. The NPC character held onto it as Tiffany fashioned it in place.

When that was done, the NPC avatar disappeared, and the girl walked over to a table with blueprints laid out. She looked at the directions and then wrote some figures on scratch paper before heading back to the power saw.

Jupiter walked over to the blueprints, impressed that she could understand the instructions enough to move on to the next steps. Even if the feel of the machinery was different, it was clear that she had skills that most people her age did not have.

This was more than a game, more even than a simulator. This was a safe way for on-the-job training for a variety of skills. The implications of which were limitless.

With that thought, another portal appeared, and Jupiter stepped back into the classroom, leaving the teenager to her infatuation.

Chapter Twelve

There was only one portal left in the classroom. Jupiter stared at it for only a fraction of a second before they stepped through, excitement now outweighing the anxiety.

They found a black space filled with scrolling lines of computer code. Each time they moved their head, their mind saw yet another stream of code running through the air like they were the intro credits to a science fiction film. Jupiter could not see anyone else with them.

"I know you're there," the voice was young, probably a teenager, but it had a mechanical feel. "They told me you might stop in. Don't worry; the others didn't know, not specifically."

"Who are you?" Jupiter asked. "Where are we? How do you know I'm here?" Their voice drifted, like escaping into an endless void.

"My name is Sammy," the voice said. There was a pause just

long enough for Jupiter to wonder if Sammy was waiting for them to speak. "Since you can't see my nameplate, my pronouns are he/him." There was only a tiny pause before he talked again. "I use an Augmented Assisted Communication Device. This means that my voice is synthesized, and there may be pauses in communication as I speak."

Jupiter waited, now understanding the variation in speech. That line was preprogrammed; they were nearly certain. He had probably had to use it every time he tried to communicate with someone new, the monotony of having to explain yourself repeatedly like they had to do with their pronouns. They waited, observing the lines of code flash by the pattern, almost soothing to watch.

"This is my world," Sammy said. "It is a program I am working on for my high school senior thesis. I could feel it when you entered. It disrupted the code."

"You can feel code?" Jupiter couldn't keep the amazement out of their voice.

"I'm not a programmer," he said. Then, after a pause, he continued. "There are programmers. They can probably feel code. I could see your code show up in the program. I have the prompt screens open."

"What are you creating?" Jupiter asked, their mind trying to grasp the current situation of two massless beings talking through a void.

"I am working on," he said, "improving AAC. So not many pauses. Also, better voices."

"What kind of voice would you prefer?"

"This is some white kid. I want the voice of a black teenager."

The phrase came instantly, meaning it had to be saved for easy reference.

"I think you have an amazing senior thesis. I am excited to see what you do."

"Good. You're helping me."

"I would love to, but I haven't been hired yet," Jupiter said.

"Yes, you have. You're here, so you're hired." The words came out with slight pauses in between like he was speaking word by word instead of a whole sentence at a time. Jupiter's mind tried to understand what he meant. Before they could formulate a reply, he was speaking again.

"To be hired, you have to be compatible. That is all they needed from you. He thought you might make it hard on yourself and asked me to look out for you, to help you get to him if you made it my way."

"Compatible? What does that even mean?" Jupiter asked, their mind swirling as they waited for a response.

"Not everyone can use the headsets. Most autistic people can, but a few still can't connect. Then there are the other people, like Stanley, who aren't autistic and can connect."

Jupiter looked around at the void of code and thought back to everything they had seen since they first put on the headset. "This whole place, it is just for autistic people?"

The answer came fast, with the words not quite matching up to the conversation, so Jupiter knew this must be another saved answer.

"Austin built this whole world just for autistic people. It wasn't on purpose; he was trying to build the world for everyone, but he used his brain as the guide. Once it was created, he tried to adapt it for neurotypicals, but he hasn't been successful. At least not yet. Even though we benefit from the full richness of AVR, what was learned in this world has been used to improve VR as a whole. It has also given us a place to learn in an environment better suited to our needs. Public school didn't even start teaching me to read until my mother fought and made them recognize my potential. However, I was given a place to find my true potential at Austin Public School. Now that I know it, I can take these skills to a traditional university to become a teacher and help other autistic kids reach their full potential."

"It sounds like someone has been working on his admissions letter for school," Jupiter chuckled.

"Yes," he said. Even though it was the same mechanical voice, Jupiter could hear the sheepishness behind it.

"Thank you for telling me about this place. Thanks for letting me hang out in your world for a bit."

"You can come here anytime," he said. "You should probably go now. He is waiting for you."

"Do you know how I reach him?" Jupiter asked.

"Go back through the portal and follow the road. Just believe that you can reach him, and you will."

The portal opened, the neon blue color was shockingly bright after the time in the void. Jupiter walked to it, almost hesitant to leave. "Thank you," they muttered.

"See you again soon." The voice drifted to them as they stepped through.

. . .

They were back in the classroom, except now it was empty. There were no longer even desks scattered about. The room looked incorporeal, like it was phasing out of existence until suddenly it didn't exist at all. Instead, Jupiter was back on the yellow brick road.

What did he say? Jupiter thought. *I need to follow the path, but I need to believe that I can find him.*

That was the key. This may all be a world uniting them somehow, but Jupiter controlled a portion of it. Now that they had beaten the tutorial and learned how to navigate, it was time to level up.

"I'm off to see the wizard," they said, laughing at their humor. Then they started to run, thinking about where they needed to be.

And the road ended. There ahead of them was a high school. It was as generic a movie high school as you could get. There was green grass with a path cut in the middle. The trail led to some wide white steps leading to the front entrance. The building itself was two stories and made of light brown brick. There were windows evenly spaced across all the floors. Except at the top of the school, there were giant white neon letters. Austin School District. It was the least subtle sign that Jupiter had ever seen, and if this wasn't a virtual world, they knew they would have been able to see it a mile away.

"I guess this is it," Jupiter muttered. They moved their hands, trying to fix their jacket and shirt, and remembered they didn't have a physical form. So they took a deep breath and pushed through the front doors.

Chapter Thirteen

The doors opened into a front office similar to the one that Jupiter remembered from their high school. There was a small lobby with short grey carpet and a scattering of blue plastic chairs. Then, there was a waist-high countertop covered in dark gray laminate. Part of the counter lifted, opening to several desks, all within view of the lobby.

A figure was sitting at one of the desks, focusing on a screen that Jupiter could not see. It looked like the avatar they had seen on Connect, but they weren't sure. They walked closer to the counter until the nameplate appeared. *Stanley (he/him)*. He seemed focused on something, and Jupiter was hesitant to disturb him. So they waited, their eyes roaming over the office space.

They turned around, looking where they had entered from. It was all glass; the steps and grass refracted as if they had just walked through the front grounds. The walls on either side were a light yellow, with motivational posters placed evenly across them.

Except these were not the posters they would have found in their school. One was a popular open-world sandbox game where a character held onto a root stuck in the dirt. Hang in there floated in the air, constructed out of building blocks. Several were just pictures of cats, no words. One had big, bubbly text in primary colors that read, "The world needs Autistics more than Autistics need the world." Behind the words was a cartoon world with a rocket ship flying away and a gray alien head in the window.

"That one was designed by one of our middle-grade students. I think they did a great job."

Jupiter jolted at the sound, turning around to find Stanley standing a few feet away. He was dressed in a blue flannel shirt and a pair of blue jeans. He was light-skinned with brown hair combed to the side. He had day-old scruff on his face like he forgot to shave.

"You can see me?" they asked.

"You're not invisible. You only don't have a defined avatar. Besides, I have admin rights. I can see everything that happens in my school."

Jupiter froze, uncertain if that was a threat or a statement of fact. Without more data, they didn't know, so they decided to ignore it. "I'm sorry if I am late."

"Don't worry about it. You finished your interview as soon as you made it into AVR. Welcome to Austin School District. I knew you could do it. I didn't realize you would make it so challenging for yourself." He moved off behind the counter, his hand gesturing to Jupiter to follow. At least, that is what they hoped he meant as they crossed to the employee section.

"Wait, what do you mean that I made it challenging?"

Stanley sat at his desk, gesturing to screens that Jupiter could not see. "There was no test. Well, I guess that is not accurate. There was a test, but that test was to see if you were compatible with the equipment. Not everyone is, not even every autistic person. Although Austin probably would have found a place for you. He felt awful about your treatment, like it is partially his fault. He tends to take a lot on himself. But everything that happened since you got here was just you getting used to things and making things harder on yourself."

His words flew out fast, making Jupiter feel like they had just understood one part before moving on to the next thought. But they were always one step behind. So they waited until there was a pause, trying to understand what he said and not just the questions swarming through their thoughts.

"I don't want you to think you were the only one that made it difficult on themselves," he continued. "One person got stuck in quicksand. I had to intervene in that one in case there were complications. It's all those movies from the 80s, I tell you. You were one of the longest and a dragon on your first trip. That is impressive. You can tell you know your way around video games. Alright, we're set up now; let's get you an avatar."

"Wait," Jupiter finally burst out. "Does this mean that I'm hired?"

"Oh, sorry. I tend to run my mouth a bit too much. Yes, Jupiter J'neii, I would like to formally offer you a position as an Educational Curriculum Consultant. The position is virtual, literally. You can work from anywhere. You will connect through the headset. I will have the rest of the work gear shipped to you shortly. I'll send over the contract so you can approve your pay."

There was a sharp ding, and then Jupiter saw a white outline of an envelope appear with a red circle around a white number one. They stared at it, trying to figure out how to access it.

"Don't worry, no one knows at first. It all connects with your brain, so think about it, and it will happen. If you're having problems, then you can use your hands to gesture. Don't use me as an example; I must gesture for everything."

The more he talked, the more Jupiter started recognizing the pauses between his words. They were brief, but they were there. It didn't help that his voice was almost lyrical, so it sounded like he was singing with a soft southern drawl at the end of each word. Jupiter concentrated on the envelope, and a screen appeared with white type on a black background.

"It's in dark mode," they said.

"Yes, everything is optimized for dark mode, as most users here prefer. It's the default, but you can change it in settings if you prefer."

"No, it's perfect. It's never the default."

"That will change here. Ninety-eight percent of the people connected to AVR are autistic; all are neurodiverse. You will find that the default will tend to be your preference more than outside this space. Is everything satisfactory with the terms of employment?"

Jupiter turned their attention back to the letter. It was a simple offer letter. They would be hired full-time as a salaried employee working virtually. Then they saw the starting pay and gasped. "That can't be right."

"If you want to negotiate, I will happily work with you."

"Negotiate?" The word was barely a whisper. "That is three times what I was making before."

"Well then, that was one more thing they lied to us about. That one may go to the lawyers as we fronted your salary for the first six months. Austin always insists that I write up the opening salary with room for negotiation. He thinks it is a good thing, but I have only had two people attempt to negotiate. So, let me change this. There, that should be correct now."

The number increased another ten percent, and Jupiter knew their mouth would be hanging open if they had one.

"So, Jupiter J'neii, do you accept the terms of employment?"

Jupiter was incapable of speaking at that moment. All they could manage was to nod their head. Stanley must have been able to see because he had moved on.

"Great, I do need your signature on some paperwork. We can do it virtually, or I can overnight the paper forms to you."

"Virtual is good," they managed.

"Excellent. I am going to send a few forms your way. Take your time. There is no rush. If you feel overwhelmed, let me know, and we can continue at a different time or in a different way. You can go anywhere you feel comfortable. It is all virtual, and no one uses this space except me, so no worries. Once that is done, we get to do the fun stuff."

"The fun stuff?"

"Yes, we get to build your avatar, your virtual you. I need to go check on something real quick. Don't worry. I'll be back." Then, without a pause, his avatar disappeared.

Jupiter sat down at one of the desks. Only once they had did they realize they had been sitting the entire time. If they concentrated, they could hear someone opening their door and the shuffle of feet above them. But that world was only there if they tried to notice it. Even now, Jupiter could swear they were starting to smell the distinct odor of bulk cleaning supplies. Every minute they spent here, the world was becoming more real. All it would take is for them to sign these papers, and they would be able to enter this world daily.

With a thought, Jupiter opened up the first document.

By the time they had finished signing their agreement to not talk about proprietary data or sharing their equipment with anyone, Stanley was back.

"All done," it wasn't a question, as the documents had all returned to him. "Let's get started."

A platform appeared, Jupiter stepped on it, and a light started to glow where they were standing. They suddenly felt like they were stepping onto a transporter platform from Star Trek, about to be broken into molecules and reassembled somewhere else. But instead, the basic form of an avatar started to take shape. It was a relatively accurate representation of the body Jupiter survived within each day.

"How do you know what I look like?" Jupiter hoped he wouldn't pick up on the disgust in their voice.

"The system does use some web-based open-sourced pictures. The headset you are using also has basic tracking abilities to help navigate. In AVR, and especially at work and school, it is required to use an avatar that resembles your physical self. You can make minor modifications; if there are reasons for an exception, they are mostly approved."

Jupiter looked down at their body. They didn't mind that they had curves as long as those curves stayed off their chest, and they wished their face was a little less round and a little more androgynous. But their body was still just as wrong here as in the real world. They felt the frustration build up in them and were sure that tears must be leaking out the side of their eyes as they tended to do.

"Like I said," Stanley said, his voice softer and slower than usual, "you can make some modifications to ensure your avatar more closely represents your gender. Why don't you work on adapting it, and you can ask me any questions you may have? The computer knows your correct gender, so you shouldn't have any problems, but if you do, just let me know, and we will work through them."

He looked at them and slightly nodded before moving over to his desk, giving them privacy. The settings were pretty standard to other avatar-building software that they had used. Except instead of having to choose a body type, there were individual settings for everything. It didn't take long before Jupiter flattened their chest and slightly tweaked their face. Just like they imagined it would change if they ever got on low-dose testosterone. Just as suddenly, they realized that they would once again have insurance.

When they were done, they pulled up a three-way mirror. They still looked like themselves. But they looked like a correct version of themselves, and for the first time in forever, Jupiter felt like they could take a full breath of air.

They looked through the clothes, throwing on a hoodie and a pair of jeans. They put on some basic tennis shoes, although they were tempted to see if the software would let them walk barefoot. Finally, they were done. They were perfect, curves and all.

"Did everything work out?" Stanley asked.

"Yes, it's perfect."

And the smile on his face was so genuine that some part of Jupiter knew that he understood what it meant to finally find yourself.

"I put in an order for the rest of your equipment. You will have some new AR glasses, headsets, gloves, and body gear delivered in a few hours to have them for your first day tomorrow. If you are good to start tomorrow, we didn't discuss your start date."

"Tomorrow's fine, but I already have a headset."

"That's the demo headset. It is the one we send out for testing. The full version headset only goes out once a person has signed an agreement. You can keep it as a backup but don't sell it, and don't give it away. Don't let anyone else use it without permission from Austin Technology. If any of the equipment is lost or stolen, let me or the company know immediately."

"I um …" Jupiter said before their words were lost.

"I don't mean to scare you. I need you to know that Austin is very protective of his equipment. If something happens that is an accident, he will understand. If it was on purpose, he is not as understanding."

"I won't give it to anyone." They wondered if Stanley saw the guilt in their face that they had thought about doing that just hours before.

"I know you won't. But I have to tell you."

Jupiter nodded in response.

"What time do you plan on working? I don't need exact hours. I want to ensure I am focusing my hours during that time."

"What time should I start work?"

"Hours are fairly flexible except for meetings. They are harder as we need a lot of different people from all different time zones. Teachers tend to have set hours since they interact with the children. However, students tend to work at different times. Many of the staff and older students tend to be more nocturnal. We think of ourselves as a 24-hour school. You can even work weekends if you want. If you work less than 30 hours a week, you may go into review to ensure you are meeting your goals. You may be asked to work less if you consistently work more than 45 hours. Autistic burnout is something Austin is adamant about preventing as much as possible. I'm going to take a guess that you prefer to be awake later. Maybe a flexible noon start time? That is about two my time, so that will work out perfectly."

"I don't have to be at work until noon?" They knew the words sounded stupid as they left their mouth, but their brain was still trying to catch up with everything Stanley said. He talked so fast.

"If you want earlier or later, that's ok. Let's play it by ear … I mean, let's use these next two weeks to figure out the best hours for you to work. I work too much; don't use me as an example, so I will ensure I am around at least some period of the day to ensure that you are oriented to your new role.

"I just log in? And I'm at work? Where is the actual school? Where are the students?" The panic was sudden but expected. So much had changed, and they had just been given everything they could ever imagine wanting. It was a lot to take in.

"Don't worry. We will go over more tomorrow. I think today was long enough. You shouldn't work full shifts in AVR, especially during the first two weeks. If you have any questions or the equipment doesn't arrive, then you have my number; message me."

"Thank you," Jupiter said.

"Anytime. To exit, take off the headset."

Jupiter reached up and was about to pull it off when Stanley spoke again.

"One more thing. Welcome to the family."

The words echoed inside of Jupiter as they pulled the cover off the AR glasses. The world was bright, and the white walls pressed in on them. The last rays of the evening sun broke through the edges of their curtains with the intensity of headlights. The room felt both unending and claustrophobic at the same time. Their body was stiff from hours of being forgotten more than usual. But Jupiter couldn't help but smile. *Family*, they were once again part of a family.

Chapter Fourteen

Jupiter stood frozen, looking at the boxes that filled their living room. The bottom package was so large that it had arrived at their door on a dolly. When it was left, Jupiter had to crouch down to shuffle it into their apartment enough that the door could close. It wasn't heavy, so much as awkward, and Jupiter was much better with a game controller than lifting.

Now, the packages were stacked, taking up the space from the end of their bed to their beanbag chair, filling the little walking space they had. With them stacked, they looked almost like a tree, one made out of presents waiting for them to dive in and destroy the packaging. But Jupiter could not bring themselves to do it.

They aren't presents, Jupiter scolded themselves. *These are for a job. Open them up.*

Before they did, they grabbed their phone and snapped a picture to remember the moment. Picking up a dull steak knife, they tore through the paper tape, exposing the first package.

AR glasses. A set designed to work as a stand-alone system.

Then, the second package. Gloves. Ones that were more than just cloth, more like a highly flexible metal.

Then, a new virtual reality headset. This one looked like a cap with just a thin piece of plastic covering the eyes. It was light and surprisingly stable on their head.

The biggest surprise of them all, the last and biggest box contained a full-body haptic suit. Except it wasn't just one suit; it was pieces that could be worn based on how immersive you wanted to be. Jupiter pulled out the card and read:

Visual - Start here, and wear your gloves.
Lightly immersive - Put on the vest.
I'm here but just from the waist up - Put on the shirt.
I am all in - Wear the shirt, pants, and foot slippers.

The material was lightweight and silky. There were no tags or seams anywhere. There was a metallic sheen, almost like the material was sewn out of metal. They were sized, and Jupiter was not surprised that Stanley had sent the correct size for their frame. What did surprise them was that there were two shirts. One shirt had a built-in binder. The other had less chest compression.

Jupiter held up one shirt in each hand, gazing at them. They were unsure what was more overwhelming that they were sent both or had both to send.

It didn't take long to get the new headset ready. Whatever configurations were set up the day prior must have been saved in an online profile. The headset greeted Jupiter by name and immediately dumped them into the head office of the school.

The room was empty, with no sign of Stanley sitting at his desk. But the room itself had changed from the day before. It was clearer and more immersive.

Jupiter was sitting on their bean bag with just the gloves and the headset on. But that world already felt like a forgotten realm. While they were in the office, it was reality. They went up to the counter, putting their hand against it to try and lean past to see if Stanley was somewhere hidden, but when their hand made contact, they felt the countertop press into their palm. They felt the coolness of the laminate.

They walked over to the chairs and reached out, feeling the hard plastic with the slightly raised surface and the cold, smooth metal of the frame. It was similar to the laminate but different in a way that Jupiter could not articulate, the same way that they couldn't if they were outside virtual reality. They moved about the room, reaching and feeling everything they could find, running their hands over smooth posters and the course carpet. Finally, they pressed their palm against the front glass windows.

"I see you arrived," the words were spoken softly, but they caused Jupiter to jerk their hand back from the window and turn to face the speaker. Stanley was leaning against the front counter. He looked like yesterday, exactly like yesterday, with his hair precisely the same, the same forgot-to-shave look, and the same blue flannel shirt and blue jeans. Except today, Jupiter realized how tall he was. He towered over Jupiter's 5'7" frame.

"You must be at least six-three," Jupiter said. "Is that real, or is your avatar taller than you are?"

Stanley's face froze enough that Jupiter realized they had said exactly the wrong thing. "I'm sorry. That was rude of me to ask and none of my business." Jupiter bunched up their hands at their side, relieved that they could feel the pressure and satisfaction they got when they did the same action in real life.

"It is quite all right. I know your question came from a place of curiosity, not malice. Everyone here has the same requirements for their avatar, even Austin himself. Our avatar represents our actual self. Now, shall we get started on training?"

While Stanley moved on from the conversation, Jupiter remained stuck. They saw themselves repeating the question about his height and the obvious reaction by Stanley. It played on a loop in their brain as they continued with the day, always there in the background. All the things they could have done differently, how they should have stopped their mouth from saying the words in the first place. But as they continued, they tried not to focus on those thoughts; they tried to remain in the present.

"First, you must learn how to pull up your menu. It should respond to a simple thought command." He was back to talking fast as if it was a race to get all the words out first. But he had to pause to make gestures to open up his menu, and Jupiter's opened up as soon as they thought about it. The menu looked similar to most game settings. It was transposed over the world, with a semi-transparent background and words written in bright lettering to help it stand out.

"Great!" Stanley took off speaking again. "Messages can be accessed in virtual reality or augmented reality. Much of your work can be accessed in augmented reality, so don't feel like you should always be in AVR. For the first week, I would recommend no more than 10 hours. Maybe 20 if you acclimate fast. We tend to use a quest system for our employees, which is not dissimilar from what our students use. Most employees respond well to it, but we can modify it as needed. Pull up your task menu."

An unrolled virtual parchment appeared in the sky with several tasks written on it. "This is the same quest menu from yesterday," Jupiter said.

"That is not surprising," Stanley said. "Everyone's system looks different based upon the input from their brain. There are basic styles programmed into the system. Since you pulled this up yesterday, the system probably marked it as your default. You can change it if you want."

"No way, this is perfect." Jupiter read down the items on their list.

LEARN ABOUT THE SYSTEM.

VISIT A CLASSROOM.

SPEND SOME TIME IN AR.

"Every day, what I need to do will appear on the list?" Jupiter asked. "I wish the rest of the world was like this place."

"Trust me when I say every new employee has said the same thing." Stanley turned to face Jupiter. "Austin built this world to be a haven for neurodiverse people. It started as Austin's idea of utopia, but the rules have changed to accommodate the uniqueness of each person. We do not follow the same rules. We know that our employees are passionate about their work, and we trust them to do it. If they can't, we know we haven't given them the tools to succeed, and we make a plan."

"I won't let you down." Jupiter felt that promise harden inside of them, filling every aspect of their soul.

"I am not worried," Stanley said. "Now, how would you like to go and visit a classroom?"

Jupiter had visions of the concrete walls and attached desks like the classroom they had seen during their interview. Instead, Stanley threw up a portal and let them into a room filled with cushions and bean bags. There were a few desks set up and lines of bookshelves. The carpet was red with primary colored shapes placed randomly around. The space was open; Jupiter could not find a single wall. When they looked, there was always something off in the distance. If you didn't like where you were, you could always find something better.

"This is our main common room. There are two others, one for students under fourteen and one for fifteen and older."

A lanky teenager was lying in a giant bean bag chair, earphones placed over...*Henry (he/him)*...his ears.

"The earphones are symbolic. It means they are listening to or watching something on a flat screen. We won't hear it since the audio is localized."

"This is where they do schoolwork?" As they continued walking, Jupiter noticed kids of various ages. Some were sitting on chairs twirling around; their eyes focused on something Jupiter could not see. Others were lying in hammocks or wandering around in circles. "Do they have full gear? Do they have the same sensory experience as in a hammock outside AVR?" Already, they found themselves trying not to say the "real world" as AVR seemed more real than any place they had been before.

"The students here," Stanley said, "are either working on less interactive parts of the curriculum. Or they are here because they want to be. The school is always open, and students can attend whenever they like."

"They just come to hang out?"

"Indeed, would you not have come here if that had been a choice? This is a safe place from the world around them. People understand them, and they have access to resources they may not have in the world outside."

They walked past a playground where two elementary school children played on the equipment. They were near each other but not interacting.

"Where is the supervision?" Jupiter had yet to see adults other than themselves.

"We will go there shortly, but first, I want to show you this."

They had made it to a large space filled with tables. At one of the tables was a group of students ranging from young middle school to high school. The students each held virtual cards and laid them down in a fashion that Jupiter did not recognize.

"They formed the club and made the game entirely on their own. The game has moved outside the school and can now be played at the adult recreation center."

They stepped closer, and the silent group could now be heard. Jupiter watched as the children played. When the youngest child had difficulty, one of the older children helped. When a teenager stood up and started moving their body erratically, the only comment was someone telling them when it was their turn. There was laughing and snorting and even voices that were too loud for regular use.

Stanley touched Jupiter's shoulder, causing them to flinch in surprise. "I think we should go meet the teachers now." Another portal had opened up, and they both stepped inside.

There were twelve teachers and thirty-three aids currently working in the teacher's lounge. It was a sizeable virtual room, not unlike the children's common room. There were more desks and chairs here, but there were still a large number of beanbag chairs and pillows. Hanging in the middle of the room was a board showing the name of each staff member and what they were currently working on. Next to it was another list that held student names. There were two hundred and twenty-three visible.

Jupiter's eyes opened wide as they saw the long list of student's names. They were written in tiny font with a symbol next to them. A few of them were highlighted in yellow or red. If they hadn't been numbered, Jupiter would have no idea how many students there were. They were trying to understand what they saw when they heard a new voice.

"Hi, Stanley told me to be expecting you today. What do you think of it all?"

Jupiter turned and faced the voice…*Janice (she/they)*…She was shorter and curvier than Jupiter, with short red curls crowning her head. Their voice was high and excited, precisely the voice Jupiter would expect was used to talk to younger children.

"The world is amazing, but this, I don't know how you understand any of it."

"It takes some getting used to. We don't use the big board all that much. It is just there for emergencies. Each of the aids has students that they monitor to make sure everything is going okay. Teachers mostly work on lessons and help students understand the concepts. Most of the kids are independent learners."

"That is what Stanley said about the employees."

Janice let out a loud laugh. "Well, I'd say that is right. After all, we aren't all that much different than the kids. Most everyone here is autistic, and we work much the same way."

Jupiter looked around at the large room. Not every staff member was here, but there were still quite a few. *They were all autistic. Of course, they are. They would have to be. But...*"I've never seen so many autistic people together in one place."

"That is the beauty of the internet. It does bring us all together, and we don't even have to change out of our pajamas to do it." Janice laughed again as they spoke.

"Janice is one of the faculty leads. She manages the elementary school faculty. There is a middle school lead and a high school lead, but they work on a rotating schedule to ensure that one lead is available at all times."

"I get the day shift because more of my kids are on at that time."

"Where are the kids?"

Janice glanced at Jupiter and then threw up some screens. "They are all in their space working on their lessons or waiting until it is time for them to be picked up."

"No, I mean. Where are they not in AVR?"

"Oh, well, some of the students study from home. They have to have a caregiver around unless they are older. But there are satellite centers around the country. Most only have a handful of students. A lot of my kids go to those. There are staff on the outside to help make sure they are safe, but their education all happens here. You have no idea how happy we are to have you here. We've done our best with the 500 current students. But with the expansion next year, we will need a more definite curriculum."

"I'm happy to be here to help," Jupiter said as their insides felt like they were swimming. They still didn't quite understand how they fit into this whole world. But the more they saw, the more they knew they wanted to find their place.

The first week of work went by fast. Jupiter spent the time trying to get orientated to the school district. They met with teachers and shadowed students as they went about their lessons.

The more time Jupiter spent in AVR, the more they didn't want to leave. Six-hour days turned into eight hours, and by the end of the second week, they were only logging off to sleep and eat. Although, sometimes they even stayed in while they ate.

The first time Stanley pointed this out, a treadmill showed up at their door. They pushed over their bed and used the space between that and the kitchen wall to set it up. Every day on their task list, they were required to spend at least an hour walking. It worked well as they paired it with the tours they were doing of the other curriculum. Instead of just thinking about walking through the enchanted forests or historical sites, they actually walked.

They constantly wore full-body gear, and the school building had become more real than their apartment.

Chapter Fifteen

After two weeks, Jupiter went to make lunch and found that they had eaten the last of their food sometime the day before. They had stopped knowing what time it was. Instead, they ate when hungry and slept when they could no longer keep their eyes open. Every few days, they would have to spend an hour offline while they waited for their headset to charge. They wandered around their apartment, pacing the small space until it was finished.

It had only been two weeks, but their apartment had already become their sanctuary, and they needed to leave it so they didn't end up starving.

They peeled off the virtual reality suit and threw it on their bed to air out. Then they braved their bathroom. It felt like an eternity since they had last looked at themselves without the covering of their avatar. But as they gazed in the mirror at their unkempt self, they were no longer disgusted by what they saw. It was the same body, but they knew it contained a version of their true self. A self that they were now allowed to be without restrictions.

After showering, they threw on their binder, a garment they had also gone without for weeks, and a t-shirt that declared in pink, white, and blue letters, "It's great to be trans." Picking up their canvas bags, they headed off to the grocery store, more sure of themselves than they had been in a while.

Venturing out into the outside world was disconcerting. No tasks were hanging over their head, and they could not control the environment around them with a thought. The world felt hollow, like it was an echo of what it could be.

Also, it stank. The air outside had a hint of smoke from the nearby oil refinery. The bus reeked of body odor combined with the stench of perfumes. Over time, Jupiter's brain had learned to add scents to the virtual world enough to make it seem real. But it was nothing like the overwhelming stench of the outside. Even the grocery store stank. There was a sweet scent of produce combined with cleaning detergent.

As they reached the shelves, pulling down food that would be easiest to eat in AVR, they realized they were happy. It wasn't just that there was a smile on their face or even the anticipation of going back to work. They were happy in the moment, picking food off a shelf, knowing they belonged somewhere where they were not picked apart for just being.

They were piling a few boxes into their hand cart when they noticed the employee staring at them. He was about Jupiter's height but a bit younger, with ginger hair and freckles across the bridge of his nose. He stood with his hands on his hips and a scowl on his face, not even pretending to be doing another task. Jupiter had gotten too used to being able to let their guard down. They had forgotten to pay attention to the people around them. They dropped the last box of Pop-Tarts in their hand cart and headed to the checkout.

"Can I help you with anything today, *ma'am?*" The last word was said with a hiss and the sharp pain of being misgendered sliced through Jupiter.

"I'm fine," Jupiter managed to say. It came out as a whisper, causing the man to smile. Jupiter tried to step around him, but he moved over, blocking enough of the cramped aisle that Jupiter could not walk around without bumping into him.

"Are you sure, *ma'am?*" He glanced down at their shirt as he said this, clearly reading the message. "I would hate for a beautiful woman like yourself to have difficulty."

He said each word with a smile that grew bigger the more that Jupiter shrunk into themselves.

"I'm fine," Jupiter pushed the words out at a normal volume, even if they were a bit shaky. "I'm just checking out now." Jupiter used their free hand to indicate the direction to the cash registers, hoping he would move and let them through.

Instead, he stood there. "Are you sure there is nothing that I can help you with? *Ma'am.*"

Tears started filling Jupiter's eyes, caused by frustration that this man had gone out of his way to make them feel unwanted. They didn't bother answering him again. Instead, they turned around and headed in the other direction.

Except his slimmer frame slid past them, blocking them off again. "Is everything alright, *ma'am?* If there is anything I can do to help, just let me know." The smile filled his face, his pleasure at their discomfort evident.

Jupiter closed their eyes briefly, took a deep breath, and then turned and walked in the other direction. They made it a few more steps before the man was in front of them again. This time, he had stopped next to a display that was talking up part of the aisle, and the only way around would be to walk through him. Jupiter looked around, trying to decide on the fastest way out of this situation, only to notice that an older woman was now watching behind them. Knowingly or not, she had her cart turned to fill the entire aisle.

"Please, just let me check out," Jupiter pleaded.

"Oh no," the clerk said in mock sincerity. "I didn't mean to make you uncomfortable. I hate to see women cry, especially in a grocery store."

Jupiter put their hands on top of their ears, the handbasket wedged on the crook of their elbow. They no longer wanted to hear the things this person had to say. Instead, they wanted to be back home in the safety of their apartment, logged back into AVR in a world where people didn't say hateful things just because they were different.

When Jupiter felt a hand squeezing their shoulder, they screamed, but it helped them realize that they had been rocking on their feet, moaning to themselves. The man was standing there looking at them, a look of horror on his face, like Jupiter wasn't even a person but some diseased being. It was a look Jupiter had seen too often. They dropped to the floor and curled into a ball, the basket falling beside them. They rocked back and forth with one long scream emanating from their mouth.

"Ma'am, you need to get off the floor," a new voice said.

"I. AM. NOT. A. MA'AM," Jupiter let the words out with their scream.

"You must get off the floor before I call the police."

The fear of that word tugged on Jupiter. All the hurt and anger was still there. The world was still too much, but some part of them knew that things could get worse if the police became involved. But they were stuck in the aisle. They wanted to leave. "He won't let me leave," Jupiter pointed at the ginger-haired man.

"I saw it all," the older woman started speaking. "The boy wasn't doing anything wrong. He was trying to help her, and she started to freak out. I don't know why they let people like her in the store. He was so much nicer than he needed to be. I wouldn't have been that nice, that's for sure."

The tears started flowing down Jupiter's face again.

"He wouldn't let me walk away. He just kept walking in front of me, asking if he could help me and misgendering me. He did it over and over, and I just wanted to get away."

"Now, now," the man said. Jupiter managed to look up at him. He was in his fifties with dark skin and short black hair sprinkled with white strands. Jupiter focused on the white strands of his hair as he continued talking. "He had no way of knowing what he said would offend you. I have a grandkid that's…well…different, and no one would know what words to use for them. So you can't expect this gentleman to do any different."

Jupiter thought over the situation. The ginger-haired man may have said the right things, but how he said it wasn't right. And no one would have kept blocking someone like that if they were trying to be nice. No, he knew exactly what he was doing. But

Jupiter knew that no one would take their side. They were the outsider crying on the floor. But the man was still there looking at them. "He wouldn't leave me alone. He wouldn't leave me alone." Jupiter realized they had been mumbling this repeatedly as they tried to process the situation.

"All right now," the man's voice boomed over the onlookers. Jupiter suddenly realized that there were a lot of onlookers, at least a dozen. So they put their head back in between their legs.

"I need everyone to clear out of here," the older man said.

The man left Jupiter alone momentarily, enough for people to leave the aisle. "I need you to leave the store now, or I will call the police."

Jupiter looked up and searched for the ginger-haired man. When they couldn't see him, they nodded their head in assent. They stood up and started walking towards the exit, leaving their basket of food abandoned on the floor. The man walked with them until they reached the doors. Jupiter knew it was to ensure they left, but they were also grateful. It meant that they were able to walk out without a problem.

Once outside, they wanted to stop and break down again, but it wasn't safe to do so close to the ginger-haired man. So they kept walking, trying to clean off their face with the sleeve of their shirt. They stood at the bus stop, watching the store to ensure no one came out to talk to them again. Thankfully, the bus arrived after only a few minutes.

When they made it home, they sunk to the floor, exhausted, hungry, unable to move, and vowed to spend as little time outside as possible.

Chapter Sixteen

The small studio apartment became Jupiter's haven. With the increased salary, they could have moved into a bigger space, but to do so would mean venturing out into the outside and talking to people without the boundary of their avatar.

They used their extra funds to bring the world to them instead. As long as they were willing to pay extra, they could get food and groceries delivered. Most would even leave them on their doorstep with no interaction required.

For ten to twelve hours a day, they went to work. They threw themselves into helping build the new curriculum for the following year's influx of students. They tested and tweaked the current programs and those that some of the senior students had been creating.

Their days were far from lonely. They had met several of the kids and would work with them as they interacted in their current lessons. They spent hours hanging out in the teacher lounge, learning how the school district was managed. But the highlight of Jupiter's days was when Stanley would come and check in with them. They had started eating lunch together and would have long conversations over various topics. It was less about what they talked about and more that they enjoyed each other's company.

When Jupiter got off work, they switched and spent time in the virtual world. They went hunting for zombies or exploring new fantasy worlds. A surprising amount of AVR worlds had been created by programmers at Austin Technology, mainly for the fun of doing so. Jupiter had even found a few worlds that they had put in requests to be transferred into learning programs.

When they were not in AVR, they spent time hanging out in VR. Going from AVR to VR was as abrupt as going from the outside world to VR. It was doable and enjoyable, but you had to interact with the world manually. However, there were more games and programs in VR, and Jupiter was having fun exploring them all.

But the more time they spent in the virtual world, the more their house fell apart. It became harder and harder to make an effort to even do the short walk from their front door to the dumpster, and their trash started to back up in bags by their door. Then, placing the takeout containers in the trash became less critical. They began to litter the counters and the floor.

Jupiter's hygiene routine also slipped. No one in virtual reality noticed if they had showered, and they had to wear the full-body suit every day anyway, so they stopped worrying about what was happening to their physical body. They still walked at least an hour a day to meet the work requirement; the rest didn't seem all that important anymore.

They could see themselves slipping away into the virtual world. They wanted it. They felt more real there, more free to be themselves. And the thought of leaving the safety of their space induced spikes of anxiety and flashes of the ginger-haired clerk. People outside hated Jupiter for being alive, for being who they were. In AVR, they had finally found their home.

When Stanley started sending them messages reminding them not to work more than forty hours a week, they ignored them. There was still so much work that needed to get done. Then, reluctantly, they would switch to virtual reality and play until they passed out in their headset.

When it was time for the headset to charge, Jupiter used the time to clean up their space, and they did manage to pack up another bag of trash between going to the headset and checking its charge levels. Then they were back on, safe in virtual reality.

So, when Jupiter logged in on a Sunday after a fitful five hours of sleep and was met with a red flashing message "Access Denied. Enjoy your weekend." They collapsed on the floor, tears streaming freely down their face.

Am I fired? Would they fire me for working too much? Stanley said they didn't fire people right away. They have to give me another chance.

As the anxiety built up, they put on their AR glasses and logged into their messages.

They started typing out a message to Stanley, their fingers flittering over the virtual keyboard, and then read back the gibberish of letters and deleted it. They tried again and deleted it.

It's Sunday, they thought. *Will I get in trouble for messaging him on Sunday?* But they had to know.

> Am I fired?

They finally asked.

The reply came back almost instantly, like their message had been expected.

> No, you are doing fantastic work. I need you to take a break. We will talk on Monday.

Jupiter read the message over and over again. It seemed positive, but people often lied because they didn't want to deal with something during their free time. The stress of the situation built up in Jupiter, which didn't help as they looked around their apartment and saw the filth that had piled up. They knew they should get up and clean it all. They should use this time to get everything back in order, but it was overwhelming. So, instead, they pulled the headset back on and decided to see if they still had access to the rest of the virtual world. They did.

When Jupiter logged in on Monday, they spawned in the same front office where they had started their job. The one where they had spent so many hours with Stanley, working out the plans for the next year, or just talking about nothing like two old friends.

Now, the space seemed small as Jupiter paced between the desks.

It wasn't long before Stanley joined them.

"Am I in trouble?" Jupiter asked immediately.

"No, you're not in trouble. But I am worried about you." Stanley pulled up two stools from behind the counter and moved them to where Jupiter was pacing. He sat down on one and patted his hand on the other to indicate that Jupiter should sit. However, Jupiter was too anxious to sit, so they continued to pace.

"Transitioning to working in a virtual environment can be difficult," Stanley said.

This stopped Jupiter short. They stopped pacing and turned to him. "No, it hasn't been difficult at all. It has been wonderful. I love working here. Everyone is so nice and talks to me. The kids are great, and I love knowing I am making a difference with my work. I enjoy working with you, and no one ever misgenders me. Working here is perfect, and I'm sorry for not doing good enough work. I promise I will fix whatever is wrong."

"Jupiter," Stanley said, for once talking slower. "You are doing spectacular work. My concern is that it is all you are doing. I am excited that you are passionate, but spending this much time in the virtual world is unhealthy. There has to be a balance between the two worlds."

"But it is so horrible there," Jupiter said, the words so quiet they hoped Stanley wouldn't hear them.

"Do you want to tell me about it?" Stanley asked.

Jupiter thought about telling him about what happened in the grocery store. Then they thought about how they would feel if he didn't believe them. The boy had said all the right things, and when they said it out loud, it sounded like they were overreacting. But they had been there and knew they were not overreacting. So they decided that it was best to keep that situation to themselves.

"I just got too excited," Jupiter said. "I wanted to make a good impression, so I've been working extra hard."

Stanley looked at them like they didn't quite believe that that was all, but then the moment passed, and he said, "We appreciate the work you have done. However, you will be more valuable if you also care for yourself. Your headset will have a timer on it for the next little bit. It will only be connected for fourteen hours before it shuts off for ten hours. I'm not going to limit your work hours, but I hope you will not work more than eight hours a day, nine at most. It would be best if you took time for yourself. It will also shut off all day on Sunday. This isn't a punishment. We know that we employ passionate people and that it can be encompassing when you first visit this world. This is the best way to help our employees when they need balance."

Stanley disappeared then, leaving Jupiter alone in the room that seemed to get even smaller. It may not have been a punishment, but it felt like one.

Chapter Seventeen

J upiter stared at their apartment. It was so small. The treadmill that was only used for the mandatory one-hour period was right next to their bed, blocking half the entrance to the kitchen. The beanbag, where they spent most of their day, took up the living room. The floor surrounding it was covered in take-out containers, dishes, and clothing.

They knew that they needed to clean. And they would. But it was too overwhelming. They needed to start smaller. So, instead, they decided to attempt a shower. They pulled off the bodysuit, turned on the sink faucet, and rubbed the cloth together to clean it. They squeezed on some hand soap, ensuring every part was rubbed vigorously before rinsing it off. When they finished the top and pants, their arms felt like lead weights. They threw the clothing on the towel rack, hoping their effort accomplished something. Then they pulled off the t-shirt and underwear that clung to their skin, cringing at the smell. They threw them in their laundry hamper, too empty, considering when they had last done laundry. Then they stepped in the shower, trading the pinpricks of water for the feeling of clean skin.

When they were clean, dry, and dressed in fresh clothing, they laid down on their bed, unsure how to spend the rest of the day. What they needed was a change of pace and a reward. Stanley had been right. They had been spending too much time in virtual reality. They had been neglecting their console. There were several games that they wanted, and they finally had the money to purchase them. Before they could change their mind, they grabbed their AR glasses and their wallet and left the house.

It had been nearly two months since the last time Jupiter had walked to the bus stop. It hadn't seemed so far away back then. Their breath came out shallow and fast, and as much as their anxiety had started to spike, they knew it was because they had not given their body the love it needed the past few months.

As they walked, they pulled up the bus schedule on their glasses. A countdown appeared in their right field of view, letting them know they had less than five minutes before they missed their ride and would need to wait another thirty minutes to catch the next one. Jupiter ignored their burning lungs and picked up their pace.

They arrived with just enough time to catch their breath before climbing onto the bus and tapping their glasses to authorize the bus fare. Then they found a seat in the middle, as far away from people as possible.

They had been more careful in their clothing, wearing an

oversized shirt and a jacket over their binder. They had thrown a baseball cap on top of their head. They did their best to ignore everyone around them, instead focusing on how the glasses interfaced with the world. If they looked at a building, there was an overlay with a brief history. It didn't seem to work for every building, probably just ones with something semi-important to say about them.

Jupiter did their best to concentrate on the augmented world, trying to ignore the world around them. A few seats up, someone watched videos on their phone without headphones. A few rows back, someone was listening to music. They had headphones, but the music was so loud that Jupiter could feel it pounding. In front, there was a mother with her two small children. They were talking and pointing out the window; it reminded Jupiter of the students, the ones they would not be able to see until tomorrow. They were not any quieter than the two talking excitedly in Spanish, but somehow, in the confines of their home filtered by the AVR software, it was easier on their ears. So they ignored the sticky feel of the hard plastic seats and the pull of their clothes against their skin and explored the AR world as best they could.

Jupiter had downloaded several applications to the glasses before rarely using them. There were a few games, including one that allowed them to move disks into funnels with their mind. It was a Star Trek reference that they appreciated, but the game itself grew boring fast.

Then, they found an app that they had forgotten all about. It was supposed to help to identify body language and translate it on screen. Jupiter opened it and glanced around. A gentleman was standing near the back door. The glasses tagged his face and indicated that he was upset. Jupiter hoped they hadn't made him upset. They tried to ensure they weren't humming without their knowledge, or their legs were not tapping. Jupiter was not doing that, but when they turned and looked again, the person was still upset.

It was all too much for Jupiter, so by the time they reached their stop, instead of transferring to the next bus, they paused the body language translation program and decided to walk the rest of the way to the mall.

It was only a fifteen-minute walk. And according to their glasses, they made it to the mall faster walking than it would have been to take the bus. However, when they reached the mall, their thighs were sore, and their feet screamed in pain. An hour on a treadmill was just not enough. Jupiter was going to have to do even more exercise.

Thankfully, it was still early at the mall. It had only been open for an hour, and most people had not shown up yet. Jupiter could walk down the hallways without worrying about touching anyone, and they knew exactly where they needed to go.

One of the first things that Jupiter had done when moving to Long Beach was to go and visit the video game stores. There were a few chain stores around, and as great as those were, the best store that Jupiter had found was a local shop that sold both new and used games. They had so much retro equipment and games that Jupiter had spent over an hour just drooling over it all the first time they had visited. Yet shopping was much more satisfying when you had money to buy things.

Jupiter thought about picking up an older system and some of the games they had grown up with. Then, they remembered the vivid virtual worlds they visited after work. Some recreated their favorite childhood game with Pluton, except it was Jupiter jumping from tile to tile, trying to escape the bombs. The thought of playing the same game in flat pixels no longer had the same appeal.

Jupiter finally decided to pick up a few newer games, something to do during their mandated time off, but even then, Jupiter could not find the same excitement they once had. As they brought their purchases up to the register, they realized that it had only taken them 15 minutes, a quarter of the time it had taken to get there. And they could have just downloaded the games directly on their system.

Tired and missing their house, they spent a few more minutes walking around the mall. They needed to tell Stanley that they had done something this weekend, or he would never lift the restrictions on AVR. Most shops were filled with clothing, and Jupiter looked at them disdainfully. They hated shopping for clothes. Everything was either too feminine or too masculine, and nothing fit their body frame. It gave them dysphoria just thinking about it.

Jupiter tapped their glasses, pulled up local options, and found a mall map. They looked through the stores, one worse than the next, until they found an arcade hidden in the upper top of the mall. They had no idea that it even existed. The glasses gave them directions by guiding them with a giant yellow arrow seemingly floating in midair, and Jupiter felt a pang of longing for their headset. But they found some comfort that they were still connected to a world that no one else around them could see. When they arrived at the arcade, it was dark and full of machines with flashing lights, and Jupiter loved it instantly. They would be able to tell Stanley they did something after all.

Jupiter bought a game card and went and looked over the selections. There was a whole group of games from the 80s and 90s, and Jupiter started playing them eagerly. Somehow, the pixelated screens were no longer depressing when they came in a giant machine that ate virtual quarters. Even better, the AR glasses offered a tips and tricks menu, and virtual hints would pop up when Jupiter needed them most. Virtual maps would overlay, telling them the best way to beat a level. In the fighting games, the list of all the move combinations was projected onto the screen. Jupiter felt like an arcade god, even if no one was around to watch.

When their card ran out of money, they thought about going and buying some more, but instead, their stomach reminded Jupiter that they had yet to eat that day, and they decided to go and find some lunch. They grabbed a slice of pizza and lemonade at the food court and searched for an empty table. People were all around them, laughing and talking, some arguing, but they were the only one alone. It was the first time in a long time that Jupiter felt lonely. They had felt connected in the virtual world like they belonged to something greater than themselves. But watching the people together, they realized exactly how alone they were.

A group of men, probably in their early to mid-twenties, entered the food court. They were laughing and roughhousing in a way that was inappropriate but not quite going over the line. The tallest guy, dressed in a hoodie and jeans, grabbed a guy with a beanie hat and t-shirt. The tall guy wrapped his arm around the man's neck, pulled off the hat, and rubbed his knuckles over his head.

Jupiter felt a stab of sympathy for the man in a headlock. They remembered what that was like from high school and undergrad. However, when the tall man let go, both men were laughing. The smaller man came back pushing, but all that happened was a good-natured slap on the back. Then, they both separated to go and buy their food.

Jupiter noticed that one of the pack was staring at them. He was the youngest, or at least the only one left with a baby face and no need to shave. Jupiter imagined they would look that way, with a slight puffing of the checks and sharpening of their jaw if they decided to go on testosterone.

Realizing they were still staring, Jupiter ducked their head and focused exclusively on their pizza.

They had insurance now and enough money for more than bills. They could transition if they overcame the anxiety of picking up the phone and making an appointment. They wanted to, but when it came time to act, they were so flooded with panic that they hid under a blanket instead.

"Hey, you don't mind if we take a seat? There are no more tables left." The voice was closer than the rest of the background noise, and Jupiter realized someone must be standing near them. They redoubled their effort to gaze intently at their pizza.

"Hey, it's no problem if you don't have room." Jupiter glanced up, curious how they had missed the other half of the conversation, only to realize that the baby-faced man was standing right next to Jupiter. He was talking to them.

"Oh, um," Jupiter floundered. "You can sit down. I'm about

ready to go anyways," Jupiter looked at their half-piece pizza, trying to decide between shoving it in their mouth or taking it and eating as they walked.

"You don't have to leave," he said. "You look cool, and we wouldn't mind if you hung with us."

The men started pulling out seats and sitting down. A few moved over unused chairs from other tables. There were only five of them, but they took up so much more space. So, Jupiter kept sitting but kept their eyes down, enjoying being a part of something.

The tall man and a man with brown hair and a jacket that looked like it belonged to a high school football star started to talk about music while they ate. They loudly argued over who was the greatest 80s band of all time, spouting out nothing but letters and numbers like AC/DC, U2, and REM. Jupiter couldn't help wondering what the acronyms stood for. But the conversation was loud, drawing looks from other tables, bringing attention Jupiter wasn't pleased with.

"So, man, what's your favorite band?" The tall man asked. It took a few seconds of silence before Jupiter realized that they were talking to them.

"I, uh, I don't have one," Jupiter said, hating themselves for fumbling again. When the men stopped and looked at them with stunned disbelief, Jupiter wanted to find a deep dark hole and climb into it. Instead, they started gathering their plate and napkins, preparing to leave.

"No, don't go," Beanie Hat said. "What kind of music do you listen to? We can help you find a favorite band."

"I don't listen to music," Jupiter said. They knew it was the wrong answer, even though it was the truth.

"No music? I can't imagine." This from the fifth man. He was dressed in what looked like flannel pajama pants with a Simpsons shirt. "What do you do?"

"I like video games," they said.

"Oh, that's cool. My little brother plays a game called FoxStar. The little dude is obsessed with it," the baby-faced man said.

"I just picked it up," Jupiter said, causing both men to laugh.

Jupiter felt a flush of embarrassment and stood up. "I should probably go," they said.

"I'm sorry," the tall man said. "Please don't go. We think video games are cool."

"Yeah," beanie man said. "We saw you sitting here and said that is one techie dude. We should get to know them. I love your glasses; they look expensive."

Jupiter flushed when they used their correct pronouns. They didn't sit back down, but they didn't leave either. "Yeah, they are AR glasses, augmented reality." They made sure to specify in case they didn't know. It was so annoying not to know what acronyms stood for. "I got them from my work."

"That is so cool. You must be super smart," the tall guy said. "Let me guess; you're a computer programmer or something."

"No," Jupiter stammered. "Nothing like that. I test educational video games."

"Yep, I knew they were smart," Beanie said.

"I have an idea," Baby Face said. "We should invite them to go to the concert with us."

"But they don't like music," Pajama Pants said.

"I could give it a shot." The words left Jupiter's mouth before they had thought it through. It had been so long since anyone had invited them to anything.

"That's great," the tall man said. "Can those glasses send text messages?"

"Yes," Jupiter said.

"I would love to see that."

Jupiter paused, concerned for the first time in the conversation. They didn't want to remove their glasses and let someone else try them on. What if they broke them or took off with them? "I'd love to show you, but once they are set up, they can only work with one user." It was a lie or at least a half-truth. They could have tried. It just would not have been an optimal experience. Sweat beaded on Jupiter's brow with the effort not to spout out all that information.

"You know, I remember hearing that," Beanie said. The men seemed to all shout out various anecdotes confirming Jupiter's half-truth, and they realized they must not have been after their glasses. They were just interested in them, and Jupiter overreacted. They were about to offer for them to try them on when the tall man spoke.

"Well, how about a demonstration then? If I give you my phone number, can you text me from them?"

Jupiter nodded enthusiastically, happy to be able to make up for their deception. The man rattled off his phone number, and Jupiter used the virtual keyboard to type a message. It was simple enough, one of the less impressive functions of the glasses, but the men whooped and hollered like it was some feat of technology.

"As a bonus," the tall man said. "Now I have your number to invite you to the concert."

The men left then, leaving Jupiter still standing with their empty plate in their hand. The table was covered in discarded food wrappers and used trays but the men were already gone, their voices echoing down the mall halls. Jupiter put their plate on one of the trays and began picking up the items, trying to leave the table as clean as when they first sat down.

Chapter Eighteen

Jupiter could barely sleep that night. They wanted to rush on and tell Stanley about their weekend encounter. They had gone out and made actual friends, something they hadn't even managed to do in virtual reality.

They logged on at nine, an early start, and were unsurprised that Stanley had yet to arrive for the day. But he was usually there by the time Jupiter came, around noon. So, Jupiter waited in the front office, pacing, filled with nervous energy.

They moved from one side of the front desk to the other. It was fifteen steps in either direction. Although Jupiter realized that they were not actual steps, and they remembered how winded they were after their trip yesterday.

Then they remembered that they needed to test the new jungle program. One of the Elementary school students had tried it and left because the birds were too scary. It was a great program to combine with exercise. They could do that right after Stanley arrived, they decided.

They paced some more, counting each time they stepped, but that didn't stop their thoughts from spiraling from their to-do list to analyzing the conversation from the day before.

Jupiter flushed in embarrassment with how they had stammered over their words. They came up with better, cooler lines. If they could do it again, they would be much better at acting like a human. Their thoughts flitted to the concert. They pulled up the concert information to see it was being held in the basketball stadium downtown. Then, they pulled up the train schedule to figure out how to get there. It was just one straight trip down the blue line.

They played the conversations that were yet to happen. When they could not imagine a concert, they pulled up video clips and watched what an actual show looked like. They were loud, and people stood close together, but it would be fine. It would all be worth it to make some friends.

When Jupiter was so full of anxious energy that they couldn't even pace anymore, they pulled up the time. It had only been fifteen minutes. They couldn't stay here, so they sent a message to Stanley, letting him know that they had something to share when he logged in and moved over to the treadmill to walk through a jungle.

Jupiter could not understand how someone thought this game was ready or appropriate for Elementary school students. The game had been programmed by one of the senior student programmers, and Jupiter knew that their intentions were probably good. A lot of research had gone into making sure that the animals were life-like and scientifically accurate.

It was just that they were programmed to display their scientifically accurate behavior directed toward the player. It started with birds coming and using you as a perch, which was enough to scare the young students. It progressed to being hunted by a black panther.

There was a wall display filled with notes to hand off to the programmers, ways to make the program less scary while still maintaining scientific accuracy. They were so engrossed that when the message from Stanley arrived, they jumped more than they did when the black panther pounced on them.

Jupiter invited Stanley, allowing him to join them in the rainforest. It was good to get out of the office. By the time his avatar had spawned, Jupiter had managed to refocus on everything they wanted to share.

"Guess what I did this weekend," they said.

"You played a new video game?"

"Well, yes. But I wanted to buy a new one. So I went to the mall and spent most of the day there. There was an arcade in the mall, and I had no idea. I only found it because of the map in the glasses. I played there and went to the game store."

"I'm glad you got out and had fun this weekend." Stanley looked around them at all the tall trees and leaves larger than his head. "Where are we, anyway?"

"This is the rainforest program I needed to review. It's amazing, right? I can't believe they built it so detailed. It's a little too detailed. It will have to become a bit more friendly, especially for the younger kids to use it. But I didn't tell you the best part."

"What's the best part?"

"I met this group of guys, and they invited me to a concert."

"You met people in the rainforest?" Stanley asked.

"What? No. I met them at the mall. I was eating lunch, and they sat down with me and invited me to go with them to a concert this weekend."

Stanley turned and focused on Jupiter, then with a hint of concern on his face, said, "Do you know them from somewhere?"

"No, I never met them before. The place was full, and I was by myself. They thought I looked cool and wanted to know about the AR glasses. Then they invited me to a concert with them. I met friends." Jupiter's face beamed as they spoke.

"They were interested in the AR glasses?" Stanley asked.

"Yes, they hadn't seen a pair in real life, and they were asking questions about it," Jupiter noted the look of concern on Stanley's face and continued. "It isn't like they were talking to me to get the glasses. I wouldn't let them touch them. I told them they only worked for the programmed user, which isn't true, but they didn't know that. They were cool about it. It was a way to connect since I don't like music."

"If you don't like music, why are you going to a concert?"

"They like music. They wanted to show me why it was great. I know it will be loud, and I probably won't like it, but they invited me, and it would be nice to have friends. I thought you would be happy."

"I just worry about you," Stanley said. He moved next to them and put his arm around their shoulder. Jupiter had found they didn't mind physical contact as much when it was virtual. "Not everyone is as honest as you are, and I don't want anyone to take advantage. Just be careful. Maybe take someone else with you to go to the concert."

"I don't have anyone to take," Jupiter said. The glow was gone from their face, and their shoulders slumped. "I thought you would be happy for me. I did something that wasn't video games. I put myself out there."

"I don't think video games are the problem. There are whole social clubs that are on AVR. You would probably do well to go and join one. There are many programmers, but most of them would share your love of games."

"You put me on restrictions." Jupiter pulled away from Stanley and stood against a giant tree trunk. A large snake burst out of the trees to attempt to eat them, but Jupiter pushed some buttons on the main program and froze it mid-strike.

"I put you on restrictions because you were logging too much time. You were on more than 20 hours a day. There is nothing wrong with virtual reality, but it does need to be tempered with caring for your body. You can't do that without sleeping, eating, or cleaning yourself. It wasn't anything personal or even uncommon. We have found that a lot of AVR employees have a similar reaction. Virtual reality can be freeing, and autistic individuals tend to go all in. I don't want you to think it is a personal slight."

"But I'm still restricted," Jupiter said.

"Yes, for now, you are still restricted. There is a minimum period recommended by the team of psychologists that consult on the AVR."

"Great, another bunch of non-autistic professionals who have decided what is best for us." Jupiter threw their hands up.

"Actually, like the vast majority of employees at Austin Industries, they are autistic, as well as specializing in autism. I think you could relate to that with your masters in developmental psychology. You may have preferred to focus on educational technology, while they prefer to focus on the application of technology."

Jupiter heard his words. They were a professional, and this was work, but here they were, stomping around like a grounded teenager lashing out against their father. They knew they needed to get control, especially if they ever wanted their restrictions loosened.

"I'm sorry," Jupiter said. "You're right. I need to do better. I just thought you would be more excited that I found new friends."

"I am excited," Stanley said. "Don't let my pessimism about people get you down. Just remember to look out for yourself."

"I promise," Jupiter said.

Chapter Nineteen

Jupiter was awake, staring at their ceiling, when their alarm went off. It was only ten in the morning, and they had been awake for over fifteen minutes; ten hours without AVR left a lot of time for sleep. But the alarm was a reminder that today they had a meeting that started in thirty minutes.

They slid out of bed, grabbed a pop tart, and pulled on their equipment. With such an early start, it would make for a long night, but it didn't stop the thrill when they first entered the world. With minutes to spare, they arrived in the classroom.

The room was similar in design to one of the lounges, just smaller. It was filled with bean bags, pillows, hammocks, and even a few chairs. Jupiter was set to meet with the Assisted Technology Club, a group of students who used adaptive technology for communication. The older students had been training the younger students to use the technology, and they had thoughts on how to improve it.

Jupiter was excited. They also became extremely nervous as students started appearing. They were a mix of various ages and sizes. The small students immediately approached one of the sensory spaces or started jumping and running around the room. Their mics were all on, and even though they used technology to communicate, it did not mean they were quiet. There were excited greetings between friends combined with self-soothing vocal stimulation. Jupiter, who did not have the luxury of noise-canceling headphones, adjusted the volume in the environment accordingly. Then they found the teacher, the only one sitting behind a desk.

Maria (she/her). Maria was in her mid-thirties, around Jupiter's age. She had long, straight black hair that went to the middle of her back, light skin, and a curved nose.

"Hi, I'm Jupiter. I'm here to work with your students."

"Welcome." Her voice was enthusiastic and loud, causing Jupiter to take a step back. "They are excited you agreed to come and listen to them. They have a lot of ideas. So, they may need some direction on what is worth pursuing and what isn't." Maria didn't look up when she talked. She kept her eyes on her tablet and said what needed to be said. Jupiter found it refreshing.

One of the school's tenets was that students and staff should not have to mask. Masking is a term used when autistic people put a lot of effort into not looking autistic. This was usually done for the benefit of non-autistic people and was exhausting. Jupiter had been masking for so long that they were unsure how to unmask. Every conversation had a dozen rules running through their head about how they should behave.

Maria started counting and pointing at the children in the room. "Fourteen," she concluded. "Great, it looks like everyone is here." With that, a deep tone played through the room, and while the room did not quiet down, the conversations stopped. "I have someone to introduce to you. This is Mx. Jupiter. They are here to help you with the changes you want to make to the ACC training and software. Did someone prepare an introduction to your concerns?"

One of the older students raised their hand. Jupiter turned to look and saw, *Sammy (he/him)*, a lanky teenage boy. He had dark brown skin and very short black hair. He wore a black shirt with white lettering that stated, "I am the future." He was sitting on a giant rubber ball, bouncing up and down as he waited.

"Sammy," Jupiter exclaimed. The words had left their mouth before they realized it might not be appropriate for an administrator to be excited to see a student. But a grin spread across his face, and his hand raised in a wave before he started to speak.

"Thank you for meeting with us, Mx. Jupiter." The voice was a standard male text-to-speech voice that pronounced Jupiter's title as letters. They made a point to add that to their notes. "I have a short statement prepared about what we hope to accomplish. Please let me know when you are ready."

"Thank you, Sammy," Jupiter said. "Yes, please. I am interested in your plan for the project."

Sammy smiled and started stimming by tapping his hand on his leg, radiating autistic joy. Then, his automated voice continued.

"We have two main concerns about the current training program. Our first concern is with the program itself. It is still challenging to use spontaneously, and we believe that can be improved. There is also no virtual interface. We still have to bring a tablet with us to be able to communicate. It is also not intuitive to use. There should be a better way to block information together, especially for younger users who cannot read. This brings me to our second point. We want to improve the training for the younger students. There are no interactive programs available. They have to learn with the assistance of others, which does not allow them the freedom to explore language in the same way as their peers. How the training is developed would depend on any changes to the program. Thank you for your time."

The text came out like a long string with only minimal natural pauses. It was apparent that he had composed the message before today to have it ready. Jupiter had difficulty with communication. They had often written down what they wanted to say before delivering an important message, but it was still adaptable in the moment. That hadn't always worked out to their benefit, but even then, it was still a privilege these students didn't have. With all the technological advances, Jupiter knew together they could create something better.

"Your feedback is important," Jupiter said, facing Sammy, and then they turned to face the entire class. "I am here to assist you. There is a term that you learn in business called subject matter experts. You are the experts. You have put countless hours into testing this technology, and while I can make suggestions, you all should guide this conversation. To help, I need to learn what you are currently doing. Can anyone run me through your training with the younger children?"

Three of the older student's hands shot up in the air.

"Great. I think seeing your different perspectives will be helpful. If anyone else wants to teach me, you can message me directly." Jupiter wanted to give that as an option even if none of the other students took them up on it. They remembered how the thought of volunteering paralyzed them but also hated never being included.

"For now, let's break into groups and brainstorm some ideas. We can work off this master project here." Jupiter opened a text window and shared it with everyone in the classroom. "Sammy, would you mind creating an outline of your concerns, and then everyone can group individual points under them."

The students broke up into groups immediately, and Jupiter was sure these were regular pairings. The document had already started to fill up with text before Jupiter could even move to work with the groups individually. This was going to be a bigger project than Jupiter realized, but they felt joy at knowing that they were doing something to make someone's life better in a way that they found helpful.

"You're a natural," Ms. Maria said. "Have you ever thought about being a teacher?"

Jupiter was startled at the words. They had forgotten that the teacher was even there. "No, I would hate to teach. I'm not very good with people."

"Maybe not outside, but in here you are. People tend to talk down to these kids just because they don't speak traditionally, even inside the school. You made sure they knew their opinions mattered."

"I've only used adaptive communication in passing," Jupiter said. "They use it every day. They are the only opinions that matter. I'm here to help them to build it."

"Wouldn't it be great if more people realized that?" Ms. Maria turned away and focused on her screen.

Jupiter thought back to all the times that others had told them that they didn't understand their own gender identity or tried to explain to them what autism was like without being autistic themselves. And they suddenly thought that maybe many of the world's problems would be fixed if people listened instead of assuming they knew better. The enormity of that thought overtook them for a second, but they knew they couldn't fix the entire world. What they could do right now was to help these kids. So they approached the first group and listened to what they had to say.

When Jupiter finally logged off for the day, they were exhausted and overwhelmed. The thought of even picking up their video game was too much. They just sat staring at the back of their curtains, thinking about all they had accomplished during the day. They were tired and overstimulated, but they realized they were also happy. It was nice being a part of something.

Jupiter realized they had never switched off focus mode while at work. So they grabbed their AR glasses, put them on, and saw three missed messages from Tall Boy.

He had given his name, Charles, but Jupiter had put him in as Tall Boy and figured that keeping his nickname was a friendly thing to do. Although they had put his real name in contact notes, in case they forgot—no need to call him Tall Boy in person.

Jupiter clicked on the messages and saw that the first one was sent three hours ago.

Do you still want to go to the concert?

Ten minutes later, he texted back.

> We're having problems getting tickets and
> were hoping you could help us.

Fifteen minutes later, he texted for the final time.

> Ah, well, I guess you're not interested.

That had been over two hours ago, and Jupiter had missed it all. What would they think of them after ignoring their texts? They hoped they understood that it wasn't on purpose.

> I'm sorry. I just got your message. I was
> stuck at work. I'm still interested. How
> can I help?

Jupiter read the message repeatedly to make sure that it didn't sound too desperate but also that they were willing to be a part of the group. Finally, they hit send.

Then they waited.

And they waited.

Their mind hyper fixated on all the situations that had happened. *They wouldn't want to hang out with them anymore because they ignored their texts. They wouldn't understand that it wasn't on purpose. They would never text back, and Jupiter would lose their only friends.*

Jupiter stood up, stretching their stiff muscles, and began to pace their small living quarters while tapping their fist against their leg. They remembered how the students freely stimmed. Then they thought about what the guys would think if they did it in front of them and stopped. Instead, they clenched their hands into fists and paced some more.

It took thirty minutes before they received a reply, and they could not relax the entire time.

> No sweat, man. We all got to work. So you're in?

> Yes, I'm in

Jupiter texted back immediately.

> Great! We are having problems buying tickets.

> Can you pick some up for all of us, and we will pay you back?

> We want to get as close as possible.

Jupiter stared at the text, trying to worry about the correct thing to do. They wished that Stanley was there so they could ask him for his help. But he wasn't, and they're an adult, so they would need to figure this out for themselves.

> It's no problem if you are not ok with that. We can skip the concert and meet up to do something later.

Jupiter looked at the second text. They would do something else if Jupiter wasn't comfortable paying for the tickets. The least Jupiter could do is help them out as well.

> Sure, that is no problem. I can buy the tickets.

You're amazing.

Jupiter smiled when they read the reply and pulled up the website for the tickets. The glasses used a standard web browser; only it was projected on the lens of their glasses, making it look like it was floating in the middle of their living room.

The show was almost completely sold out. There were only a few groups of tickets left that would allow all six of them to sit together. When Jupiter saw the price, they hesitated.

I can get tickets near the front. But they are $180 each. I can get some seats near the back that are only $30.

I can't believe there are still some tickets available upfront. Go ahead and buy those.

Are you sure? That seems like a lot of money.

Don't worry. The guys will be excited. Go ahead and buy them before they sell out, and I'll make sure everyone has your money.

Jupiter hesitated. The total with taxes and fees was almost $1500. They hadn't spent that much money on something ever. But they got paid more, and they hadn't spent the money.

They watched the timer tick down on the cart. Only ten minutes until the tickets would be released.

Are we set? I want to tell the guys we
have tickets.

The timer continued to tick down. They considered texting back and telling Tall Boy they couldn't buy them. But then they couldn't be trusted to be part of the group. They would continue to be alone and friendless.

The timer ticked down to five minutes, and they clicked purchase, putting in their information and agreeing to the terms of service.

It's done.

You're amazing. Thanks!

And Jupiter held onto those words as they got ready for bed. They cherished them as they checked their bank account and saw the decreased balance. Then, they told themselves not to worry. They would get most of the money back, and everything would work out okay.

The next afternoon, when Jupiter met with Stanley, they told him how they all had tickets to the concert. They decided not to share that they had paid for them and that they would get paid back. They didn't want Stanley to get concerned, especially since everything would be fine.

Instead, Jupiter put all their focus on work, at least until Tall Boy texted them again.

Can you send over the tickets?

I thought we would all meet up first and go in together.

That would be great. It's just that Nick might be a little late. I want to make sure he can get in.

That made sense to Jupiter. Of course, they wouldn't be able to make it at the same time. And they could send over one of the tickets to make sure that Nick could get in. Jupiter had added them to an app on their handheld to get scanned, but they were also sent as a printable document. They could access it that way.

I can send it over. Does he have access to pay me back electronically?

When Jupiter didn't get a reply, they returned to work. Their mind replayed the conversation, trying to understand if they said something wrong or if there was something else they were supposed to say. They finally decided that Tall Boy must have just gotten busy.

The reply came a few hours later when Jupiter was immersed in a traditional VR zombie game. It popped up in the sky, causing more of a scare than the zombie trying to eat their brains.

I talked to the guys. I'll collect the money and get it sent over to you. Can you forward the receipt over?

Sure, no problem. Will you be able to send the money to me before the concert?

Once I have the email, I can get it to you.

Jupiter pulled up their email and forwarded the ticket receipt. Then, they went back to battling zombies.

Chapter Twenty

When Friday finally arrived, Jupiter was relieved. They loved the projects they were working on, but they were having a hard time focusing. It was the first time they wanted to step away from virtual reality for a break. Although Jupiter was worried that they hadn't heard much from Tall Boy. They sent him a message when they got off work.

> Where are we meeting up before the concert?

An hour passed, and Jupiter hadn't heard anything back, so they decided to distract themselves by pulling out their gaming system and playing one of the newer games they had picked up. They played for a few hours, lost in an attempt to grind and level up their character before taking on one of the boss battles. Before they knew it, it was ten at night, and they still hadn't heard back from Tall Boy. They decided to try texting again.

> Hi. I just wanted to check on the plans for tomorrow.

The anxiety started to set in. Jupiter didn't understand why Tall Boy wasn't getting back to them. *Were they not going to show? Were they going to be left with six tickets to a concert they didn't want to see? But of course, he would text back. They wanted to see the show, and Jupiter had the tickets. He was probably just busy.*

Jupiter decided to distract themselves. They ordered dinner from a nearby spot and threw on some clean clothes before heading out to pick it up. It was just a ten-minute walk from their house, and the night air felt good, even if it did smell like smog. They had started trying to go outside more, remembering how good walking felt.

They had food and were walking back to their apartment when the text popped up. Jupiter read it on their glasses as they walked.

> Let's meet up at 6:30

Jupiter pulled up the tickets in their inbox and looked at the concert time to verify they had the information correct. The concert started at seven. It didn't seem like a lot of time to go through security and find their seats. But they were with a group now, and Jupiter knew they needed to be flexible.

> Sounds great. Does anyone want to meet up for dinner first?

They read that over, making sure it sounded casual and not

like they were concerned about the timeline. The reply came back right away.

> We might pick up something after. 6:30 is
> good.

After is good, Jupiter thought. Their mind wandered toward heading out to a spot downtown and relaying the events of the concert. They would be tired and socially overloaded, but it would help cement their friendship.

> Sounds great. What about Nick? Will he
> be able to make it then to get his ticket?

> Don't worry about Nick. He is already
> taken care of.

Jupiter wasn't quite sure what that last message meant. But at least they knew what they were doing tomorrow. They still felt a bit anxious about the whole situation, but Jupiter figured it had to do with attending their first concert. It was, after all, their first social outing with a new friend group. It was a significant milestone.

They made it home, ate dinner, and tried returning to playing. However, they couldn't focus and eventually turned the game off to go turn in early.

Jupiter woke up at eight the following day. They could not remember the last time they had woken up so early, but they were full of nervous energy and unable to go back to sleep. Instead, they went into the kitchen and cooked themselves some eggs and toast, wiping down the counters as they went. After they ate, they threw away all the food containers and bagged up their trash to take outside when they left.

Then they went and showered; the sunlight streamed through the window, but it didn't bother them today. Living day in and day out with their avatar, the embodiment of how they saw themselves, should have made living with their actual physical form worse. Except that it didn't. Instead, they learned they didn't have to think about how others perceived them. Although, they suspected a lot of that probably had to do with not being constantly misgendered.

Once showered, they put on their binder and the clean clothes they had picked out yesterday. They had no idea what to wear to a concert, so they wore jeans and a black t-shirt with an unbuttoned shirt over it to help hide their curves. They were cleaned and ready to go; it was just now nine in the morning.

Uncertain what else to do, they made their bed with clean sheets, picked up all their dirty clothes, and put them in a hamper to wash. Then, with so much time on their hands, they relented, took the clothes down to the complex laundry room, and started them. While the machines were going, they cleaned their apartment. They even took out cleaning spray and wiped down surfaces. There was so much dust all over everything, like the air was so dirty that it clung to whatever it could find.

Once the laundry was finished, they folded it and put it away. Their apartment was cleaner than it had been in months, maybe ever. It even had a slight citrus smell from the cleaner.

It was now noon. They couldn't stay inside anymore. They picked up the trash bags and headed out. The complex dumpster was in front, and they dumped their two trash bags in before looking up and down the street, trying to decide what to do. Without a better idea, they headed on their way.

They needed to take the metro rail, an above-ground subway, to get downtown. However, to get there, they would need to catch a bus. So they started walking in the direction of the bus stop. They saw one of their favorite taco spots on the way and decided they might as well stop off for lunch.

It wasn't until Jupiter finished the third taco that they questioned why Tall Boy hadn't texted them. But they brushed it off, their anxiety being overwhelmed by their excitement. They had everything planned already. There was no reason for them to reach out. So they focused back on their fourth taco and headed to the bus stop.

Jupiter had never ridden the rail line before. They had seen it as it drove down the street near their old office building but had no reason to get on. So it was like an adventure as they got off the bus and saw the platform high above the ground. They scanned their bus pass, went through the turnstile, and walked up the steps.

A few people sat on benches waiting for the metro rail. They all looked bored, like this was the thousandth time they had done this, and nothing was exciting about it. For Jupiter, it was an exotic trip. It looked like an above-ground subway, as they had seen in films. There were decorations and statues trying to make the platform look nice, but the seats were hard and covered in sticky substances, and trash littered the ground.

Jupiter checked the signs, ensuring they knew which side of the platform to get on, and waited. The train came every twenty minutes, so it would not be long before one arrived. In the meantime, they pulled up an overlay on their glasses and played an alternate reality game where they popped bubbles. They probably looked ridiculous, but it passed the time.

When the train did come, they waited for the doors to open and nervously stepped between the platform and the train car. Their overactive mind conjured fears about falling in the two-inch gap between the platform and the train. Once they were on, they found a seat in a nearly empty compartment and sat down to enjoy the ride.

Jupiter had only gone to downtown LA once. They had gone as part of a business function, taking a ride share that navigated the freeways and bumper-to-bumper traffic. They found the experience so nerve-wracking that they didn't need to go again. The metro rail was different. They did not have to worry about getting hit by other cars. Instead, they could enjoy the experience. Not that there was much to see. It was gray and black, with only a few palm trees to break it up. Jupiter didn't like their old small college down much, but they missed seeing green and nature. The only nature here was pigeons and rats. And palm trees. Jupiter did love the palm trees.

As they moved closer to downtown, the train started filling up, but it was early enough on a weekend that it wasn't too crowded. Jupiter grew bored, but they didn't start another game, too worried about missing their stop. Instead, they pulled up the train schedule and followed their progress reflected on the window as they looked out. The view may have been slightly depressing, but they didn't want to accidentally make eye contact with people inside.

When their stop came, they stood up and waited by the

door. When the doors opened, they hurried out, making sure they were not trapped inside. They were there. It was loud with cars honking, construction, and the general sound of people as they walked past on the sidewalk a few paces away. They instantly wished that they had brought their headphones. Jupiter looked around them, and then they looked up. They were surrounded by buildings taller than they had ever seen, not skyscrapers, but tall enough that Jupiter felt disoriented trying to see the top.

Once the train had continued on its way, Jupiter crossed the tracks and went to the sidewalk. They looked down at their watch. It was only two. They still had more than four hours until they met up with their friends. Unsure what else to do, they decided to at least find the area. They pulled up the directions to the stadium on their glasses and started walking.

The area was under construction, but the type with an air of permanency about it, or at least like it had been going on for a while. Plywood platforms were covering the sidewalk that seemed aged with time. It made Jupiter's anxiety spike with claustrophobia. But at least it was still light outside, even if the sun was hidden behind the buildings. The unfamiliarity of the area was overwhelming, but everyone around them seemed to find it all completely normal, and Jupiter found strangers giving them looks. Jupiter checked in with their body and realized they were gaping at all the buildings, and their hands were tapping along their thighs. They went to stop, but the image of the students' autistic joy fluttered in their mind, and they continued. They weren't hurting anyone.

It hadn't taken long to make it to the stadium, and Jupiter was happy to see so many people walking around, eager and excited just as they were, even though the concert didn't start for hours.

There were a few restaurants in the area, but it was still early, so they walked around. Unlike the area Jupiter walked through, this area was meant for gawking. They let their feet wander as they allowed themselves to relax. They were here. That part was done. Now, they just had to enjoy themselves.

Nearby, they saw a tall building covered on one side with a giant advertisement for the newest TV special. There were at least ten people hooked to scaffolding painting in the face of one of the stars. Jupiter stood watching for nearly 30 minutes. The city lost as they focused on the people, so tiny they couldn't make out any of their features beyond the color of their clothes. They manipulated paint rollers to create images right before their eyes. Until a pedestrian bumped into Jupiter, nearly causing them to fall into the busy road. They decided it was probably best to hang out somewhere else.

Jupiter was outside the main entrance at six. They had eaten and wandered as much as they could. There was nothing left to see. The area outside was emptying as everyone went to take their seats. Jupiter texted Tall Boy to let him know that they were there. It made sense that he hadn't texted back. They were probably still on their way.

At 6:20, they texted again, asking how close they were. Still no response.

At 6:30, their anxiety spiked, and they decided to go in and find the seats. They could return and meet the group with the tickets when they arrived. They pulled up the tickets and moved to the line to enter.

They held out their handheld so the person could scan it, but instead of ushering Jupiter in like they had done with everyone else, they frowned and looked at their device.

"I'm sorry, ma'am, it looks like that ticket has already been used," the person said.

Jupiter tried to ignore the gendered statement. They were confused enough about what the problem could be. "It shouldn't be used. My party isn't even here yet, and I bought them. I have the receipt." They pulled up another ticket to be scanned.

"Sorry, that says it has also been used," the person said.

Jupiter pulled up another, and when the person shook their head pulled up another until all the tickets had been scanned.

"It can't be," Jupiter said. "I have the receipt right here. I paid for them all. My group was going to pay me back tonight."

The person looked at Jupiter with an expression that Jupiter didn't understand exactly; they just knew they didn't like it.

"Did you share the tickets with anyone?"

"No, I just sent them over the receipt."

"The receipt has copies of the tickets on it. Maybe they used those to get in?"

"But none of them worked? One of the tickets was for me."

"I'm sorry, I really am. I will need to ask you to speak to customer service so I can keep letting people in."

"Of course, I don't mean to get in the way." Jupiter stepped out of line and looked around, trying to locate customer service, but mostly, they were trying not to cry. They came all this way and didn't understand what was happening. Today was supposed to have been a fun night, but it wasn't turning out to be fun at all.

Jupiter felt a tap on their shoulder. They turned and saw the ticket person. "It's right over there, hun." The person pointed, and Jupiter saw a sign pointing toward customer service.

"Thank you," they mumbled before walking away.

Customer service was the same place to buy tickets if you did not have one already. The line was at least ten people long. As they waited, they checked their texts and saw that Tall Boy had not yet gotten back to them. They would all be so upset when they realized someone had stolen their tickets. It was the one job that they had. But they figured they had better get it over with.

Something is wrong with our tickets. When I tried to go inside, they told me they had already been used. I'm in line with customer service now. They will get this taken care of. When you arrive, you can come and find me.

Jupiter was surprised that the reply came back almost instantly.

Nothing is wrong. We couldn't find you so we went inside already.

I have the tickets.

Jupiter knew it was a stupid response. Even though they didn't know why, they had the tickets. How could everyone have gone inside? No one had even paid them for them yet.

You sent them to me, remember?

Jupiter didn't remember. They had forwarded the email to him, so he had copies of the receipt. Jupiter was the one who had added them to their handheld to be scanned. That was Jupiter's job.

They scanned all the tickets. I didn't have one to use.

Sorry, Brian's girlfriend wanted to come. She must have used your ticket. You can buy another one and come hang out with us.

Right, the night could still be salvaged. Jupiter could buy another ticket. They were already in the correct line. Then, they could hang out with their friends, collect the money for the tickets, and still have a good night. It could still be a good night.

Ok, I'll see you soon.

The line moved slowly, but eventually, Jupiter made it to the front of the line. They showed the cashier their tickets. "My friends brought an extra person and used all the tickets. Can I buy something close to where they are sitting?"

The person behind the counter was a young man who looked like he had just barely graduated from high school. He punched the keyboard until he responded. "Sorry, there is nothing left down there. All I have are tickets for the balcony." His voice was nasally and high-pitched, grating on Jupiter with every word he spoke.

"I guess that will work," Jupiter said. They scanned their palm over their reader, permitting payment, and Jupiter watched forty more dollars disappear from their bank account.

They went to the closest entrance, trying to avoid the last ticket person they encountered. They handed over a paper ticket to get scanned and finally walked into the arena.

Chapter Twenty-One

The concert had already begun by the time Jupiter made it inside. The sound vibrated throughout the mostly empty halls. It pulsed through Jupiter until they could feel it overwhelming them just a few steps in. They immediately wished that they had brought their earphones, no matter what their friends would have thought.

But they had made it this far, so they had to endure a bit longer. Jupiter looked at the tickets they had first purchased and found the section number. They showed the electronic pass to the usher and walked down to the seats.

The music was loud, and Jupiter had difficulty concentrating enough even to see the little letters on the end of the stairs. Then they panicked momentarily, wondering if they would recognize Tall Boy and the guys. They had only seen them once, and even then, they had spent much of the time staring at the table.

Although, the anxiety seemed to be misplaced. Once they

found the row, the group was easy to spot. They were loud even in the middle of the chaos. Jupiter stood at the end of the row, watching them scream with the music, their bodies jumping up and down and constantly bumping into each other. Finally, Tall Boy noticed them staring. He scooted in front of a few people until he reached the aisle.

"You got in," he said. Although, he had to say it three times before Jupiter heard him. The third time, he screamed it right next to their ear.

Jupiter just nodded back.

"I need to get paid back," they said. The tears were starting to form behind their eyes, and they were trying not to let them fall. They weren't even sure what was causing them. Or maybe it was a combination of all things.

"Sure, sure," Tall Boy said. "We can do it after. Where are you sitting?"

"I need to get paid back now," Jupiter said, straining so their words reached him.

"I mean, I don't think you want me pulling out the cash now in front of all these people. You could get beat down before you reached your seat. I got it right with me. I'll give it to you after the show. We will meet up with you."

"Where?" Jupiter asked.

"We'll come to you. Just wait for us."

"I'm at the top. I couldn't get a ticket close."

"We'll meet by the front entrance. Don't leave without meeting up with us. I want to make sure to pay you back today."

Jupiter stood watching him as he left, laughing and apologizing as he maneuvered his body toward his seat. Then, he put his focus back on the band. No one turned to look in their direction again, and eventually, Jupiter moved to find their seat.

They had to go up. Then, they had to go up again until they made it to the top row of the stadium. The band looked like little action figures dancing around. While it was quieter up top, it still vibrated until Jupiter thought their bones would shatter.

Jupiter tried to watch the show. Fireworks were shooting off from the side of the stage, bright, unexpected bursts that hurt Jupiter's eyes. They appeared suddenly, in time to the music that Jupiter could not anticipate. Each time, they jumped, bouncing into the man standing next to them. He held up his beer, laughed, and danced, allowing his body to continually touch Jupiter's in small random movements.

Everyone seemed fine by this. Pulsating noise, randomly touching strangers, and bright flashing lights. Most were singing along with smiles on their faces, dancing and laughing together. A few were sitting back, enjoying the music, but everyone seemed to be having a good time. Jupiter searched the crowd, trying to find at least one person who looked as miserable as they felt. They couldn't.

They made it two songs before they walked to the hallway, tears threatening to start at any moment. They saw the t-shirts for sale with the band name and some weird artwork of what looked like someone drowning. They thought about buying one to remember the night. Then they looked at the design and decided there was no way they would ever actually put that shirt on. Besides, there wasn't much about this night that they wanted to remember. Once again, they seemed to be missing something that everyone else seemed to understand without any effort.

Finally, the music grew too much as it echoed through the hallway. They moved outside to sit next to the main entrance, waiting for their friends to come out. Maybe there could still be some salvaging the night. Once they got paid back, they could offer to take everyone out to dinner. It would help to make up for the misunderstanding about the tickets.

They sat beside a pillar, feeling the coolness beneath their skin.

"Did you ever find your friends?"

Jupiter looked up and noticed the ticket taker that had tried to help them.

"Yeah, they made it inside. You're right. They already had the tickets. I'm just waiting for them so they can pay me back."

"Next time, you shouldn't offer to pay." The person looked at Jupiter with that same expression, the one they didn't quite understand. It made them feel like they weren't a complete person, like something was missing.

"Yeah," Jupiter said. "It's good, though. There was a misunderstanding, and the music got too much for me. We're going to go get some food after."

The ticket person gave them that same look and then walked away, leaving Jupiter alone again.

They stared into the night, trying to get the ringing out of their head. Eventually, they started playing a few AR games, the playing field projecting out into the open space of the concourse. Jupiter was amazed that there was no disruption with the harsh fluorescent lighting and how it expanded the playing field to incorporate the extra space. Jupiter wanted to enjoy it. They tried to enjoy it. However, their heart just wasn't into it.

When people started leaving the stadium, they stood up.

Jupiter searched the groups of people, trying to find their friends like a lost puppy dog. But everyone just walked past, not giving them a second glance.

Eventually, the people started to exit in trickles, and some part of Jupiter was not surprised that they had missed the group. They sent a message off to Tall Boy asking him where they were. They waited until the doors started to be locked and people stopped emerging before they started walking back to the metro rail.

It was late now, nearly two in the morning, and the streets were dark, pocketed with the glow of business signs and a few apartment windows lit up. They made it back to the empty platform. They felt exposed, waiting alone for the train to show up.

It was worse when someone else joined them. They sat down on a bench near them even though there were several others to choose from. Even though they just sat there staring at their phone, Jupiter became frozen with fear.

When the train finally came, they felt relieved until they sat down and realized it was again just the two of them in the entire compartment—the person sitting only a few rows ahead of them despite all the other choices.

The city lights flashed by the window as they hurdled down the tracks, but Jupiter couldn't relax. There wasn't anything precisely wrong; it was just that everything had gone wrong. They felt out of control and didn't know what else would happen.

When the person got off, Jupiter felt some tension go, but not a lot.

The platform was empty when they got off the train. They walked down the steps, the light from the platform declining as they walked toward the vacant parking lot. A few streetlights were turned on, but most were broken, and Jupiter felt trapped in the darkness. It was an eternity before they reached the opposite side and the bus stop. Not that they felt any safer there, being completely dark.

They pulled up the bus schedule, apprehensive about how long they had to wait. Except the bus stopped running hours ago. Tears started to build in their eyes again. They had planned on asking someone for a ride home after the concert. They had figured it wouldn't have been a big deal since they all lived nearby, but now they were trapped. They could walk home for over an hour in the early morning hours. Or they could call a ride share. Neither of the options seemed like a safe idea, but they eventually decided the car was better than walking. At least they would get back to their apartment's safety sooner.

In the near darkness, their glasses still worked. The apps now showing up as bright, flat overlays hiding the night. Their request was accepted, and Jupiter tracked the car's progress and watched as headlights pulled into the parking area. The front license plate was hidden behind the light of the headlights, so Jupiter walked around back, ensuring it matched what was on their screen. Then they opened the back door and slid in. The driver seemed to match the picture. Both were Indian with short black hair and similar facial structures. Jupiter had never been good at matching pictures with actual people, but it seemed close enough. And Jupiter released a little tension as the driver greeted them and then turned around to drive.

Jupiter opened their work notes, noting that they needed to request a facial recognition program. Something simple that would help ensure people matched their pictures. With that thought, they remembered the software they had turned off on the way to the mall, and Jupiter opened up the program that helped read facial expressions. Maybe if they had kept it on, this night would not have turned out how it had.

"Did you have a fun night?" The driver asked. Jupiter looked at the profile to see that his name was Issac.

"I went to a concert with some friends," they said.

"I'm not much for concerts. The music is just too loud," Issac said.

Jupiter looked up, and the glasses caught the reflection from the review mirror. Contentment the glasses read. Under that were the green words spelling out "truth." At least one person tonight wasn't lying to them.

"It was too loud for me also. I don't think I will be going to any more concerts."

They pulled up in front of their apartment complex, and Jupiter wished them a good night as they walked inside.

Once their door closed and was locked, they flung themselves on their bed and let the tears flow.

Chapter Twenty-Two

Jupiter woke up half hanging off their bed and completely dressed, including their shoes. Even their glasses were on their face, the low power icon blinking in the bottom of the frame.

They pulled up their messages and were unsurprised that Tall Boy had not texted them. They thought about blocking the number, but if there was any chance that they could get their money back, they would take it.

Instead, they removed the glasses and put them on the holder to charge. Then, they changed out of their outside clothes and into a pair of comfy pajama pants that had become a staple.

They looked around their apartment. The one good thing that had come of yesterday was that the place was clean. It made things more bearable or easier to ignore.

Then they grabbed their video game controller, sat in the beanbag chair, and spent the rest of the day absorbed in a fantasy world where they were the long-foretold savior. A world where people liked them and the rules were explained before you ever started playing.

They only stopped playing long enough to open their door to take the food from the delivery driver. Eighteen hours later, they had beaten the game. As the end game credits rolled, they fell asleep, still sitting in the bean bag chair.

Jupiter logged into work later than usual on Monday. It was already three in the afternoon, and they were thankful they didn't have any meetings they missed.

They were unhappy to see a message from Stanley asking them to check in when they arrived. Talking to Stanley was usually the highlight of their day, but today, they wanted to stay as far away from him as possible. They didn't want to tell him what had happened. They didn't want to hear an "I told you so." They already realized how stupid they were to think anyone would want to hang out with them. How foolish they were for falling for yet another trick, only this time losing over a thousand dollars in the process. They also didn't want Stanley to think less of them than he probably already did.

But he was their boss, and they couldn't avoid him and keep their job. And they loved their job. They loved their job, not the type of love they tried to fake, but the kind that made them happy.

So, they were transported to the main office and told him they had arrived.

"Hi," Stanley said. "Did you have a good weekend?"

Jupiter looked at him, trying to figure out if he was making casual conversation or asking about the concert. Finally, they decided on a neutral answer. "It was ok. I'm glad to be back at work."

Stanley looked at them a bit too intently, and they realized they didn't fool him at all.

"You ok?" He asked.

"I stayed up too late last night playing a game. Sorry, it took me so long to get in today."

"You know the rules. As long as you get your time in and make your appointments, you can work when you want. I knew you had big plans this weekend. I thought I would check in and see how you are doing, but if you would rather, we could talk about the assisted communication project you have been working on."

And with that, Jupiter knew that he had remembered. He always remembered. But they appreciated that he was giving them an out from the conversation. That made them feel even worse for being afraid to talk to him. So they decided to tell him a condensed version of the events.

"I'm not a big fan of concerts. They are really loud, and people are right next to you the entire time. I can't believe people enjoy that. Then I didn't get home until really late. I think I enjoy visiting places virtually more. You have more control over your environment."

"How did it go with your friends?" He asked, a hint of concern in his voice.

Jupiter's face fell. All the anxiety they were trying to avoid bubbled to the surface, but they didn't want to tell Stanley exactly how much they had failed. "I don't think I will be hanging out with them again."

"You're ok, though? No one hurt you?"

Jupiter felt the tears in their eyes again but forced them down. Crying in VR glasses was messy. "No one hurt me. I wasn't even with them. I'm fine. I'm stupid, but I'm fine. They had me pay for the tickets, and I believed everything they said. How dumb can I be?"

"They had you pay for the tickets?" Stanley moved closer, hesitating, waiting for Jupiter to nod assent before he put his arms around them. Jupiter felt the weight of it pressing down on them, and for the first time all weekend, they didn't feel so alone. He waited, letting them get themselves composed.

"Alright, let's get some work done," he said. "But remember, this isn't anything that you did wrong. It is on those bastards that took advantage of you." That was the last he said on it as they moved on to talking about the project.

Jupiter tried to let it go, to move past it and focus on the people relying on them, but they couldn't. Once again, they had allowed people to take advantage of them. They couldn't let it happen again.

Chapter Twenty-Three

J upiter started setting alarms again. There was an alarm to remind them to wake up at ten every morning. Then, they had an alarm to remind them to eat breakfast and put on clean clothes for the day.

They set alarms to remind them to work out, shower, and eat lunch. Then, there were alarms to remind them to stop working, eat dinner, and get out of virtual reality.

They realized that they needed the alarms to help them remember and that they were not the enemy. They still had a schedule that worked for them and found themselves happier than they had been.

Once they got a handle on the basics, they added time to go outside daily. They got into the habit of walking to one of the restaurants to pick up lunch. They added a reminder on their work headset to stand for so many minutes a day.

Eventually, they regained full use of the VR headset, but it didn't matter. Well, except that it allowed them to go on the headset on Sundays now.

They had no designs for extensive outdoor excursions. The small ones suited them just fine. Most of their needs were met in virtual reality.

At Stanley's suggestion, they planned to visit some of AVR's more social areas and interact with people. Except they were nervous, unable to lurk as they had once done. So they put it off until, finally, Stanley volunteered to go with them.

"Technically, I'm allowed to go," Stanley had told them. "The AVR works for me just fine for some reason. But I have tried to respect the space. Sometimes people need a place all their own, and they don't need people like me bursting in."

"Yes, abled cis white guys tend to take over every space," Jupiter said.

Stanley paused, his hand in mid-motion to adjust his virtual hair, a habit Jupiter assumed was from the outside world, but he didn't say anything.

"I'm sorry," Jupiter said. "I meant it as a joke. I didn't mean you took over every space. I just meant in general. And I didn't mean I don't have my privilege."

"Jupiter, you're fine. I'm not upset. I was thinking. But it doesn't matter right now. Let's go hang out and have some fun."

So after work, they both transported to The Autistic, one of the more popular general social clubs. They had both agreed it would be a good place to dip Jupiter's toe in the socializing world.

Jupiter had realized through their years that being autistic did not mean that people were introverted, especially as introverted as they were. Sure, they were all socially awkward, but some autistic people seemed to thrive off the energy of others. They managed to interact through all the social awkwardness and even have friend groups. It baffled Jupiter, who often found they could be invisible in a room full of people.

The Autistic was nothing like what Jupiter had expected. When Stanley had said club, they had pictured dancing and music and people bumping into each other. The club was lit, well enough to see without difficulty. The walls were a dark gray with some textured grey shapes etched into them. As soon as Jupiter arrived, they were presented with a menu. The environment was completely customizable. You could change the brightness of the lights or the color of the walls. You could not only control the volume of your environment; you could mute it entirely or only mute out music and loud sounds. There were also status updates you could select. Green was, *everyone is welcome to approach me.* Yellow was, *I'm open to social interaction, but I need space also.* Red was, *please do not approach.*

The club was divided into separate rooms, except that there were no physical barriers. Each room was separated by what Jupiter could only describe as a force field or loading zone that kept out the environment from the other rooms.

"Where would you like to go?" Stanley asked.

Jupiter pulled up the map. There were two dance rooms. One was titled "I Want to Feel the Energy," and the other was titled "Dance Bubble," which mentioned each avatar would have its own dedicated dance space. There were rooms for tabletop games and card games. There was a karaoke room and a conversation room that mentioned that you could tag some of your favorite topics to talk about. There was even a library. Jupiter had a hard time imagining that there were that many people who attended the club to utilize all the rooms but supposed that they all didn't have to be occupied. Although they had never visited a club that was this advanced before.

"Do you like board games?" Jupiter asked.

"That sounds like fun."

Each room was connected, and while you could walk from one room to the next, there was a navigation option at the entrance to the club. Jupiter walked over to the game room icon and found themselves instantly transported to the new room.

The game room was spacious, with at least twenty tables to sit around and play board and card games. There were another ten long tables that could be used for tabletop games. Each table was spaced far from the other, with the long tables having even more room for the players to lounge around. Two intense-looking tabletop games were being played. Each had a bubble over the space, sealing them off from the rest of the room. There was a third table with a few people hanging around. Except this one was not sealed off. Instead, it had a sign hovering in the space above that said *Warhammer 40K* and beneath it, *open for casual play*. Six smaller tables were closed in their bubble, and a few more were not sealed off. Only three of those had signs above them, one looking for Magic: The Gathering players, another looking for Dungeons and Dragons players, and a third just said it was open to playing whatever.

Off to the side of the room, there was a bar and a snack shack. Someone was behind the bar making drinks. Jupiter guessed it was an NPC, a nonplayable character, but then maybe it wasn't. Perhaps someone just enjoyed mixing virtual cocktails.

Jupiter sat down at one of the tables, and a virtual menu appeared, allowing them to pick from any of the programmed games. There was also an option to put on a privacy bubble or put a call out for new players. As soon as Stanley had sat down, Jupiter pressed to put up a privacy bubble.

"What would you like to play?" Jupiter asked.

"Do you play a lot of tabletop games?" Stanley asked.

"No. I know about them, of course, but I've mostly just stuck to video games."

"I saw that there was a video game room. We could go there if you prefer," Stanley said.

"I… Maybe I'll visit it next time."

Stanley nodded in acceptance and didn't push further. Instead, he looked at the menu of game options.

"Have you ever played Uno?" he asked.

"Yes, that game, I know." Jupiter laughed.

They played a few rounds of Uno and then found a deck of playing cards where they started out playing War and ended up making up their own game with rules so complicated that neither of them understood them. While they played, Jupiter watched the room around them. There was never any pressure to do more than what someone wanted. A person came in, a red aura hanging off of them, letting everyone know not to disturb them, sat down at a table, and pulled up an NPC to play a game with them. Then they left. Another party had people coming and going. People walked into their game, talking like they were old friends and leaving. But Jupiter could not hear any of it through their privacy screen. It was a place built for them.

"Thank you for coming with me tonight," Jupiter said. "I

know you probably had better ways to spend your evening, and I appreciate it."

"I had a lot of fun. It has been a while since I have hung out in AVR for anything besides work. I appreciate you inviting me along."

Jupiter was pretty sure that he meant what he said, even though they both knew that he was doing this because Jupiter was too awkward to do this on their own and too scared after what had happened the last time they had tried to make friends. They appreciated it all the same.

Jupiter started visiting The Autistic on their own after work. They didn't go daily but paid a visit when they wanted to be less alone. Although they always set their status to red, they did try visiting some of the other rooms and seeing what else the club had to offer. Once, they sat down to a storytelling competition, and a fellow red sat near them. Neither of them talked to the other, but it was like they were enjoying the event together, and it felt great. One day, they knew they would come in and set their status to yellow. Maybe they would sit at one of the conversation tables and find someone who wanted to talk about video games. Or perhaps they would sit at the card game table and find someone who wanted to play a game with them. Just knowing that they had that option made them feel a little lighter. But for now, they used all their socializing energy at work, interacting with the AC project that was still ongoing or trying to socialize with some of their co-workers. But they had hope that one day they may finally find a friend.

Chapter Twenty-Four

It wasn't unusual for Jupiter to not see anyone at work for long periods, especially when they were working on a specific project. But it was uncommon for Stanley not to attend one of their scheduled meeting times. They were supposed to review the final notes of the AC project. The kids had come up with some fantastic ideas, and Jupiter had refined them into an action plan moving forward. They needed Stanley's approval before returning it to the class for their final input. It was the most exciting project they had worked on, and they were bursting at the seams to show Stanley. Except he was late.

Jupiter clicked to open their messages and saw nothing. They sent Stanley a second ping, but it went unanswered. However, they noticed that the student's communication feed had over a thousand new notifications. They stayed off the channel, as it was used mainly by the kids and contained a lot of cat gifs and fart jokes. But the feed was sending a new message nearly every second, and with nothing else to do, they switched over to see what the kids were talking about.

There was a gif of an anime character turning red with anger.

> Does this mean they are going to close the school?

> No way, Mr. Austin will never let them do that.

Then, a gif of an animated cat with large tears flying out of its eyes.

> Why do people have to be so mean?

The messages kept coming, but now Jupiter was confused. *What had the students so concerned? And who was talking about closing down the school?*

They switched over to the employee chat, but it was unusually quiet. A message hadn't been sent in over an hour. So, Jupiter pulled up Stanley's profile and saw he was in one of the meeting rooms. Jupiter checked their calendar, but there was no meeting they had missed. The meeting room was not locked down, so Jupiter transferred themselves over. They spawned right next to Stanley.

The room was full of students and staff. Large screens were being displayed across the room. They all showed a white guy talking at a large brown pedestal.

"They are taking our kids and turning them into mindless zombies. Soon, we will all be part of the machine's agenda," the man on the television said.

"What is going on?" Jupiter asked Stanley.

"That's the governor of Texas. He is talking about the school. He's calling for it to be shut down." Stanley's attention stayed focused on the screen as he talked.

"They bring your children into this cult, and make no mistake; it is a cult. They are indoctrinating them young to keep them loyal to their cause," the man continued.

Jupiter had heard these words continually throughout their life. Every time someone had tried to claim that being transgender was unnatural. The political rhetoric mainly quieted down once federal laws had been passed, guaranteeing national protections for trans individuals and federally recognizing the nonbinary gender code. It hadn't stopped the hate, but it stopped it from being a political talking point. Jupiter continued listening, trying to understand how anything he said could be applied to the school.

"They keep you out by saying that your brain isn't right for the technology to work while they hide in their club, plotting to overtake the world. Austin Technology is the largest technology company in the world, and they hire within, giving jobs to graduates of their school instead of hardworking Americans. This is why I am introducing bill 51c to stop the indoctrination of your children and bring Austin Technology's action into transparency. The exclusionary technology will be banned, and schools must be held in person as God intended. Once I am elected to the Senate, I will bring this same bill to be enforced nationally. We must save our children. God bless."

The man turned and walked away without answering any questions.

"Most of the world didn't even know we existed, and now he

painted a target on our back so he could be elected to the Senate," Stanley said.

"I don't understand," Jupiter said. "How could he have been talking about Austin Schools? This isn't a cult. It's just a school. And what does he mean about God wanting students to meet in person? God didn't create that system; people did. Even neurotypical educators recognize that it is an outdated system that needs to be updated to appropriately educate our students for the future."

Stanley turned away from the screens, now muted with closed captions as journalists discussed the governor's words. "It isn't about being factual or accurate. It isn't about what is best for people at all. It's about fear. They need someone to fear. So now that they can't legally hate trans and queers, they decided to focus on autistic people." His hand reached out like he was punching something Jupiter couldn't see. "They always attack the children, the people that legally don't even have a way to fight back."

Jupiter was struck by the passion in his voice. Even though he wasn't autistic himself, this school was his world.

"I know firsthand what hate can do," Jupiter said. "My parents were the ones threatening librarians for having queer books and voting for making being transgender illegal. When they found out I was trans, well, I didn't think I would walk away alive. I'm lucky they just kicked me out with the clothes on my back. They can't do this to these kids. But they aren't alone. Austin Technologies is too massive a company to go against. If nothing else, he can buy his way out. Right?"

"I hope so. I really do."

The news conference was all anyone could talk about. The student's chat became a mess of gifs and anxiety that even the moderators couldn't keep up with. The staff mostly stayed in the gathering room, talking amongst themselves and trying to figure out the best way to help the students. Everyone was walking around either in shock or radiating with anger.

At least until an hour later, when Austin's response was issued. He didn't bother with a press conference. Instead, he dropped a video directly to the people on all his social media accounts.

"I believe Governor McTilen is very mistaken about the nature of Austin School District." Austin was framed vertically, focusing on the upper half of his body. He wore his trademark black t-shirt with brown hair styled in the boyish cut he was known for. He stared intently at the screen, his face exhibiting little emotion. "We are a national charter school that works with students with autism spectrum disorder. I have been very open about my diagnosis and experience in school, and I wanted to give back. That is why I started this nonprofit educational system. These are all students who were not able to succeed in a traditional school setting for various reasons. With the help of a care team, which includes their guardians, they are flourishing. No child has to stay. We are not a cult. We are a school that follows a mandated curriculum. Yes, many of the students do go on to work for Austin Technology, but this is a good thing. These students would have been written off as unemployable, existing on disability benefits. Instead, we help them have a career they choose, where they can live their lives with self-sufficiency."

The video was only a few minutes long, and after it had finished playing the first time, it played again.

"That should help, right?" Jupiter asked.

"I just don't know," Stanley said.

Jupiter opened up a screen, looking at the news feeds. Many were taken with what the governor had said. There were already opinion pieces about why the school must be closed down. Positive articles were hidden in the masses, saying people were overreacting or bringing attention to blog posts made by autistic individuals who talked positively about the school. A prior student also had an interview about how the school helped them set up an independent art career. But these were all hidden among the articles with catchy headlines like *The Cult School* or *Will Your Kids Be Next?* and the fear that never entirely left Jupiter alone began to expand in their gut.

Chapter Twenty-Five

That night, Jupiter was too restless to be left alone. They thought about taking a trip to The Autistic but ended up in one of the traditional virtual reality worlds.

Jupiter had visited this game many times in the past. It was a virtual world where you spawned into a main social room but then went off to play mini-games. You were alongside people and could communicate with them, but you didn't have to. It was exactly what they needed. So they decided to play a game called Space Shotput. It was a pretty basic game that still had graphics that glitched. It was more apparent now that they had spent so much time within AVR how less-developed traditional virtual reality was.

The object of the game was easy. You spawned in with a group of five to eight players. Everyone had a laser gun that you used to shoot at moving targets that looked like cardboard cutouts of aliens. The person with the top score was the winner.

Users could talk through a mic, but Jupiter preferred to stay silent. They weren't the only one. There was usually a whole collection of "mutes", as they were called. However, the majority of players seemed to have no problem speaking. Sometimes, the language was vulgar, but usually, it was just trash-talking about how the person would win. The players ranged in age from elementary school to players in their fifties or sixties, and Jupiter always tried to remember that everyone on the other side of them was different. They could have silenced their speakers and not heard anyone, but usually, they felt better being connected.

Most days.

Today, it was not working out at all.

"Did you hear that the governor of Texas is trying to ban virtual reality?" the voice was that of an adolescent.

"Nah, he only wants to ban AVR tech," this from a deep voice of an adult. "And he should. It isn't right that those no-gooders think they can horde the good tech for themselves. He should share the damn tech so that everyone can use it. Damn cult."

"Didn't you see Austin's video?" another user asked. "He said it isn't a cult. It's a school. I heard there wasn't a code to use the headset. You have to be autistic to use it. That is why some of the streamers could get it to work."

"Yeah, you noticed how the streamers who get it to work suddenly stop streaming," the younger player said. "It is a conspiracy. You shouldn't have to be a r— to get it to work."

Thankfully, the speech filters ended up silencing that word. Jupiter hated it.

Unfortunately, the talk didn't end once they loaded into the game. Even the traditional smack talk had turned into a conversation about AVR.

"I'm going to f— you up like a crazy AVR user," was the first smack talk line uttered as the round started.

"Nah, you aren't good enough to be AVR," another said. "You're just a poor peasant VRer. Only elite players get the good tech."

"Don't b— s—- me. You don't have AVR tech. Why would someone with that kind of gear be playing this hack game? They can play the real games where you can't tell reality from virtual reality."

"I heard you can even have s— and it feels like the real thing," a third voice said.

Jupiter tried to filter out the conversation and enjoy the game. *Maybe they were right. Why were they hanging out in this virtual world when they could return to AVR and play in a much better environment?* They had just wanted to escape from it all; they knew the club would be talking about nothing but the announcement. They didn't expect it to be all anyone talked about here.

When the game ended, and they loaded back into the lobby, Jupiter was pulling up the menu to leave when they heard part of another conversation.

"The solution is simple. We should wipe them all off the planet and have nothing to worry about anymore. We don't need people like them."

Jupiter heard the words and froze. They were the exact words thrown at them all their life. They heard it all growing up when people called them out for being queer before they even understood what that meant, before they even understood that other people felt an attraction to one another. They heard it when they were first diagnosed as autistic before they could talk and later when they couldn't respond to the world as others expected. They had to fight for the right to exist when other people took their existence for granted. And they had taken it and would probably have continued to take it, but these words were directed toward kids. That was horrible enough, but these people were talking about Jupiter's kids. The kids had spent months working on improving software to speak more fluently. Who just wanted to be able to make friends, buy groceries, and have a job that could cause them not to live in poverty. These kids came from diverse backgrounds of every race and socioeconomic status. They were queer and straight, trans and cis, but they were all neurodiverse, and that was enough to call for their death?

Jupiter felt their hands clench, and their pulse started to race as they thought back to one of the histories they read during grad school that documented the death of neurodivergent children during the holocaust by doctors, doctors that would then go on to be revered as saviors. Their people had gone through trauma, trauma in addition to the racism, sexism, and genderism, that some also had to deal with. They often didn't have family that even understood this trauma, and at times, like in Jupiter's case, their family was part of the problem. This small handful of children had found a place to be themselves. To express their autistic joy and not have to conform to the world was enough for this adult stranger to call for their death, and Jupiter had had enough.

So, instead of leaving, they walked over to the avatar that said the hateful words.

The avatar was a human-sized frog. It was animated and

bright green with a bright yellow belly. The voice was masculine and middle-aged. Jupiter took all their fury and spoke for the first time in this world.

"Please do not say such horrible things." They hated how their voice came out weak since traditional VR was missing the audio features they used in AVR to make their voice sound more gender-neutral.

"Oh, look at you, being called out by the child," this from one of their friends dressed up in an avatar of a scary clown holding a cleaver.

They both started laughing hysterically, but Jupiter held their ground.

"Those are people you are talking about. They are children, and I heard you talking about extinguishing them from the earth. Who talks about children like that?"

"Oh, please," the frog said. "It isn't like they would let me kill them. But you have to admit that this world would be better off if we did not have to continue pouring resources into them. They are a dead weight in society. They should shut down the school and move on."

"You don't want these students to be a drain on society, but you also want to shut down the school that is helping them to be successful? The school teaches them how to get jobs, make money, and find happiness. Isn't that what everyone wants in life?" Jupiter's voice was getting stronger as they found themselves on sturdier footing.

"What good has any of them autistic people done to society? They take taxpayers' dollars and take away resources that the rest of us need," Frog said.

"What have they done?" Jupiter asked in disbelief. "They have given you this. You sound old enough to remember the old virtual reality, the worlds so pixilated people routinely got seasick and the headsets so heavy you felt their presence constantly. This world was created by the neurodivergent. And maybe this world is not as detailed as AVR, but that is just a hiccup for now. Those kids you complain about will graduate and work on improving the next generation of headsets until you can enter the virtual world and forget that you are even there."

"I think she may be one of them," the clown said.

"They," Jupiter said. "My pronouns are they/them. They are right there next to my username for anyone to see. So you are either purposely misgendering me to be hate-filled, which is on brand, or you are stupid."

"You're both autistic and trans?" the frog said with venom. "How dare you even talk to me."

Jupiter's hands clenched into fists, and they tried to take a deep breath before their words got entirely away from them. They knew they were being provoked and wouldn't take the bait. Maybe these two would not listen, but they noticed that the lobby had grown silent. At least forty avatars were staying to listen to how the conversation would play out. Maybe someone out there would understand what they were trying to say.

"What have you ever done that is so great?" Jupiter asked.

The frog and the clown both turned back to them. "I don't have to answer to you," the frog said.

"No? You are so busy claiming that some elementary, middle, and high school students have not done enough to deserve their place in this world. I'm just curious what you have done to earn your place."

"I deliver pizza," the clown said.

"Don't speak to her," the frog said.

"Pizza," Jupiter said. "That's a great job. I bet people are excited when you drop off a nice hot pizza when they are hungry. It means they don't have to cook. I bet you bring a lot of joy into their lives. I know I'm happy when my pizza arrives."

"If they are so happy, they should tip more," the clown muttered. "If it's such a great job, I should get paid more."

"I bet it sucks when people undervalue what you do for them," Jupiter said.

"What?" the clown said.

"Oh, stop talking," the frog said.

"Do you like delivering pizza?" Jupiter asked.

"No," the clown said.

"But I bet you work hard at it," Jupiter said.

"I do."

"It must be frustrating when people do not realize how hard you work. You deliver their pizza on time and still hot, and then they don't even tip you. Or the company you work for relies on you to deliver their food so they can get paid, and they don't even pay you enough to afford your own place to live."

"Wait, how do you know I don't have my own place?" the clown asked.

"Dude, you deliver pizza for a living. Of course, you don't have your own place," the frog said.

"So here is my question for you," Jupiter turned and looked at the clown, making it a point to ignore the frog. "Why are you so angry that a group of kids that attend school virtually and have no connection to you at all exist? Why aren't you angry instead that you can't make enough money doing a job that is important to help you do whatever you want to do?"

"I don't know what I want to do," the clown said.

"Will you just shut up," the frog said.

"There is nothing wrong with delivering pizzas if it makes you happy. But if you want to do something else, then maybe figuring out what that is should be the next step."

"You're right," the clown said. He moved closer and hugged Jupiter, and to their dismay, the program was sensitive enough to movement that Jupiter felt the contact in their haptic shirt. But they sucked it up and reached around to return the hug.

The clown logged off and disappeared from between Jupiter's arms.

"What the f—," the frog said. Then he continued on a tirade that Jupiter decided they did not want to hear and logged out themselves.

Chapter Twenty-Six

Jupiter woke up to their alarm and started in on the morning that had become routine, checking their accounts as they ate breakfast. There wasn't usually much to do, but it helped them clear out anything from the day before.

They were surprised to see a text from Tall Boy, the first text they had had sent the concert.

> Way to go. You tell them!

Jupiter read it over and over, trying to understand what it meant. Finally, they decided that he probably had texted the wrong person. Jupiter thought about using it as an opening to ask about their money again, but they had already given up on it, and they didn't want to reopen that awkward chapter of their life.

Then they noticed the messages on their non-approved list

were in the thousands. Their account must have gotten on some massive spam site, but they didn't have enough time to go through and block them all. They would have to do that after work.

Jupiter finished their breakfast and switched out the AR glasses for the virtual ones.

They spawned in the meeting room where they had logged off yesterday, except they were not alone. The room was still crowded, and the screens played yet another video. Jupiter tried to brace themselves for another new horror when they looked up and saw themselves, at least their virtual self.

There they were, standing next to a neon green frog with pink neon spots and a killer clown. The volume was off, and the words were displayed with closed captions, but Jupiter did not need to read what was said. They were there. The only question was what everyone else was doing seeing it.

See me

Stanley's message popped up as urgent, and Jupiter found themselves full of despair. This was how it started before they told you that you had made a big mistake and let you go. But there was no point putting it off.

Jupiter pulled up Stanley's profile to transport them, except they were not in the office spawn point. Instead, they were in some room called The Office, as if it was the only one in all virtual reality. They clicked transport and found themselves in a large corner office with windows overlooking a forest that was too bright green to be authentic. Jupiter turned around and saw a large brown desk with two chairs in front of it. Stanley sat in one of the chairs, and the second was open, waiting for Jupiter. Behind the desk was Austin.

They hadn't just been summoned to the principal. No, they had been brought to see the head of the whole company. Then, with a sigh, they moved and sat in the chair. There was nothing left to do but face what was happening. They couldn't go back and change anything, and they weren't sure they would even if they could.

"Do you know why you are here?" Austin asked.

Jupiter realized it was not a rhetorical question; he was asking if they knew why they were here, and part of them relaxed at least a little.

"There was a video playing in the meeting room," Jupiter said. "Someone must have recorded what I said."

"Have you heard of a streamer called JollyTime?" Austin asked.

Jupiter shook their head. They didn't keep up with streamers; they just enjoyed playing the games on their own.

"He was doing a live stream last night when he picked up someone saying some pretty hateful things. I'm not sure why he would choose to stream that. I'm sure it was for the views. I've read over some of the comments, and it was extremely active. Except then, he captured someone confronting them, someone who may have well admitted that they were part of AVR. They posted the conversation as a separate video and VRvid. The video has over three million views already. It has been picked up by most of the local news stations. By the end of the day, I'm not sure anyone online will not have watched it at least once."

Jupiter was sure that their face must be colorless under their VR glasses. They did know that their hands were shaking. "I understand," they said. "It's just that someone needed to speak up for those kids. You heard what they were saying. No one needs to know what it is like to hear those words at that age."

"I assure you, Mx. J'neii, everyone in this room knows what it is like to have such hateful comments turned towards them." Jupiter turned to Stanley, wondering why someone would have spoken a death wish to him, but Austin continued talking. "I have been very open about my own experience in school. I would not have survived it if it had not been for Stanley. However, I did speak out. I posted my response, which was created using a whole team of professionals to address the situation. That message has been overshadowed."

"That message didn't work," Jupiter said. "I'm, I'm, I'm sorry." Their words dissolved into a stutter.

"No, please continue. I am interested in hearing what you have to say."

"The message wasn't working." The words were spoken slowly like there was a block keeping them inside, and then the dam broke, and the words came pouring out. "At least not in the virtual reality world. They are jealous because they think they are locked out of an exclusive club and want in. There is so much secrecy behind AVR, and I'm unsure if that is on purpose or because it has been created to help with sales. But they see this place as an elite institution that will solve all their problems, and they have been denied entry. These same people who have every door open to them whether they want to take the door or not."

"So you are saying we should bring back the narrative that

autism is bad? Should I tell them they don't want to be here because it would mean they are broken? Of course, they are excluded; it wasn't on purpose but a happy accident. We have a space where we can finally be at peace."

Jupiter turned to Stanley before responding. Except his face was impassive, and he was looking at the ground and not at either of them. Jupiter wondered if he was even there or if he just popped up his headset and decided to sit this meeting out, but then they rebuked themselves. Of course, he wouldn't do that.

"AVR is everything you said. I couldn't agree with you more. And no, we won't win this by their narrative that being autistic is miserable. We need to show them autistic joy. We need to show them how much this world means to us. But that won't be enough. We must make this about them because they don't care about anyone else."

"I see your point. I appreciate both your enthusiasm and your dedication to the students. I hope you will trust that my team and I have the situation underhand moving forward. I'm not sure more viral videos such as this will be good for the long term of the school or the company."

Jupiter sat there uncertain. It seemed they were being dismissed, but they couldn't be dismissed, not yet. He hadn't fired them. "Wait, you're not firing me?"

"Not at all. You may have been a bit enthusiastic, but mostly, you were the product of bad luck for doing the right thing. Besides, we need you here to make this place better. Stanley has kept me updated on your work. You are doing an excellent job."

"Thank you. Please trust me that it was not my intent to

become viral. I don't do well with people. I don't usually speak online. I just couldn't let them stand there and say those hateful things. And everyone was letting them. It was horrible."

"I understand," Austin said. "I am sure this whole thing will blow over quickly."

"I had better get back to work," they sputtered, uncertain how to leave gracefully. Finally, they just pulled up their menu and selected the top choice to depart. They materialized in the main office, and Jupiter took a deep breath, their body shaking with relief. They could have lost all this because of two trolls. They were still shaking when Stanley appeared.

"How are you doing?" he asked.

Jupiter couldn't answer. They couldn't quite catch their breath.

"It's okay. You're okay. Just breathe in and breathe out. You can take the headset off."

Jupiter shook their head adamantly. "No, no, no, no."

"It will be fine. You can come back later after you have calmed down. Or you can take the rest of the day off if you need to."

"Please don't make me leave," Jupiter spit out before going back to trying to catch their breath.

"You don't need to leave. This is your home."

At that, Jupiter started crying, snot blubbering out of their nose and tears leaking out the corner of the glasses. They were loud and messy, but at least Stanley could only hear the breakdown and couldn't see it. All the pain and hurt they had tried to bottle down for the last thirty years had finally tipped and come to the surface. It all exploded. But Stanley stood beside them patiently until their wracking sobs turned into sniffles.

"How are you doing?" Stanley asked.

"I'm a mess," they managed to answer back.

"It is okay if you log off and come back on."

"I almost lost it, all of it. I don't even know what happened, not really. I couldn't imagine having to give all of this up."

"No one is taking this away from you," Stanley said. "You are not fired. Austin wasn't even upset. He is just trying to keep the situation under control so it doesn't impact the school or the company. A lot is going on behind the scenes that you don't see."

"You mean he is buying people off?"

"He is engaging in politics. He isn't all that great at it either, but he has a team who are."

"I'm just worried. It may be good to throw money at politicians. But that doesn't impact the people. I don't think you know how bad it can get. After I was outed by one of my teachers, it got bad, really bad. I don't want our kids to have to go through that."

"I know," Stanley said. "One day, I will tell you exactly how much I understand, but for now, we just need to trust that money and power can do more than we can now. Our job is to be here for the kids. You can listen and help them, and we will make sure that ASD stays the safe place it has always been. You are an important part of that. I'm not sure you realize how much the kids here love you."

"I love them too," Jupiter said. "I'm going to go clean up, but then I'm coming back on to get to work."

"That sounds great."

Jupiter took off their VR glasses, which were now slimy to the touch. Thankfully, the tech was lightweight and easy to clean, all thanks to autism ingenuity, even if the neurotypicals didn't recognize that. They wiped down the glasses and their face and looked at themselves in the mirror. They were no longer that scared, defenseless high school student. Maybe they didn't have life figured out, but they could at least be there for the kids.

They put back on their headset and returned to work.

Chapter Twenty-Seven

It was a tense week at the school. The message boards were a constant stream of conversation. The students were worried, except they weren't even sure what they were concerned about. The virtual world seemed divided between AVR and VR. While traditional VR users could not enter AVR space, AVR users had regularly gone to VR worlds. A lot of them were programmers for VR or, like Jupiter, enjoyed the diversity of games. Except now the chats were a lot of conversation about AVR, almost all of it negative. Austin had issued a statement asking employees not to speak publicly about the situation and reminding them about the nondisclosure agreements that everyone had signed.

The school had also been directly impacted; a few students had even been unenrolled, although thankfully, it was not a common reaction. Most of the students had already been failed by traditional schools when they arrived at ASD. There was no place for them to go back to.

The staff was also worried. The chat was a constant barrage of news articles about calls to close down the school, and attacks were starting on individuals who were autistic or perceived to be autistic. It didn't seem to matter that they had no connection to the school; that wasn't the point. The issue was a war on people who were not the status quo.

An autistic teenage boy and his mother were beaten while grocery shopping. Autistic individuals were getting evicted from housing without legal notice. Late-night talk show hosts were decrying the violence while making fun of being autistic. Jupiter wanted to hide from the outside world even more than they already did.

They tried to keep busy working long hours, logging off, playing their video game console, or going to bed early. They tried going out, but their avatar was enough like their physical self to be recognized, and a swarm of people descended on them for autographs. They ran away, going home the long way like some lousy movie in case they were being followed. Now, they ordered in and always wore a face mask and a hat when they opened the door.

The video kept making the rounds at work, also. The kids had been playing with the videos, adding sound effects, text, or their thoughts, and were sharing it regularly in their chat. Staff Jupiter had never met would spawn next to them and talk to them like they were famous. They had become a minor celebrity. The video was one of the most viewed in history and was regularly played by both sides of the debate. Even within AVR, Jupiter was swarmed anytime they tried to visit a world. Eventually, they were given special permission to use a different avatar for off-work hours.

Jupiter just tried to keep their head down and focus on their work. They tried not to call any more attention to themselves, hoping that whatever Austin was doing behind the scenes would start working because the world seemed even more dangerous than when they had gone off on the streamer. But Austin was a visionary with a plan that had built an entire tech company, the most significant since Apple and Google. Jupiter just had to have faith that he was doing something to help.

The only person who did not treat them any differently was Stanley. He would still ask how they were doing, but it was the same type of concern he had before. He didn't bring the conversation to anything happening unless Jupiter mentioned it, something they did not want to do. Instead, they focused on work and the kids.

"I think we should have groups for the kids," Jupiter said in one of their meetings.

"Groups about what?" Stanley asked.

"Their chat is filled with anxiety and fear. Why not give them a safe place to express it with people who understand?"

So Stanley set up a group. To be safe, he had students get parental permission and brought in the psychology team and the school counselors. When Stanley suggested that Jupiter start the group talking about their experience, Jupiter wanted to decline. But it was their idea, and if they wouldn't speak, then why would the kids?

But when the day happened, and Jupiter found that they were standing in front of over a hundred children, they couldn't stop their hands from tapping their legs with anxiety. They looked out into the group of children, most of whom were on a bouncy ball or a hammock. A few were even sitting on special chairs, allowing them to put their heads toward the ground. Jupiter stopped worrying about what their body was doing and went up to speak.

"Hi," they started. The students let out a loud cheer that filled the entire space, and Jupiter felt the nerves leave them entirely. "I thought it might be a good idea to come here today to talk with each other. A lot is happening in the world right now, and it can sometimes be scary. But we are lucky that we have each other. Does anyone have any questions they would like to ask or anything they would like to share?"

The room wasn't quiet. The kids did not sit still or have to stop making noises. But no one volunteered to talk.

"That's alright," Jupiter said. "Why don't I go first? I am not very good at speaking. Sometimes, what I am thinking won't leave my mouth. I go silent when I want to tell someone they are not being nice."

"But you stood up to the bullies."

Jupiter did not know where the voice originated, so they tried to respond to the whole room.

"I did. I think my words worked because I had a superpower that day. Do you want to know what it was?"

"What is it?" a few kids asked.

"I want a superpower," a girl in the front said.

Jupiter looked at the girl when she spoke. "My superpower is you." Then they talked to the whole room. "When I spoke up, I could do that because I thought of all of you. You have taught me so much since I joined you, but the most important thing you have taught me is that I am so happy to be exactly who I am. With that power, I was able to speak up. But so many times before, I couldn't. And you know what? That is okay also."

"Were you scared?" The question was asked by, *Jacob he/him*, a boy with red hair and glasses who looked down at his knees as he spoke.

"I am scared a lot. But when I spoke, I wasn't scared, or I wasn't scared for myself. I was scared of what would happen if what they said happened. That fear helped my words."

A middle school boy, *Tommy he/him*, with brown hair and a green hoodie, raised his hand.

"Yes, Tommy." Jupiter recognized him from the AC club, and they waited while he finished his words.

"People look at me weird when I leave the house. They always have. They speak like I am not even there. But recently, it has gotten even worse. My mom is even scared to let me go on errands with her after my twin brother got in a fight at school because of what someone said."

Jupiter waited for the psychologists or councilors to speak up, offering these kids wisdom. When they didn't, Jupiter offered what they could.

"People made fun of me for being Autistic when I was younger, but it wasn't until people found out that I am nonbinary that I was ever terrified of being who I am. I learned it was important never to be alone, but sometimes you had to push past the fear. The hard part is knowing when that is. Unless our parents are also autistic, they may not understand, but your parents love you and want everyone to be safe. And you have everyone here also. Your friends understand, and the staff once was a young autistic person, even at a different time. You can always tell us anything; we will do our best to help. I want each of you to know how important you are to me."

When Sammy raised his hand, Jupiter gestured to him. He had been working on a message, and they had been using his communication unit to test some of the improvements, so he spoke a little faster and, with Austin's expedition of a voice actor, now had a voice that better matched his identity.

"I live in a rural area. My mom has to drive an hour to get to a center that I share with one other kid, but she does it because even before now, I wasn't safe at school. At least it was safe at the center, but now some people are showing up holding signs with angry things. There are security guards that help us drive through the mob. My mom is afraid, but I'm staying no matter what. I'd stay home, but sometimes I still need help, and my mom must go to work."

Jupiter stood frozen, uncertain how to respond. They didn't know that it had gotten that bad. Anger grew inside them that such a remarkable young man had to experience such hate, but also anger that Austin hadn't used his influence to fix the problem. Before they had to find something to say, another student started sharing their experience, and then another. They stayed together an hour longer than scheduled so that everyone would have a chance to be heard.

Afterward, Jupiter went to find Sammy, he was hanging out in the AC meeting room.

"I don't mean to disturb you," Jupiter said. "I just wanted to make sure that you are okay."

"Thanks," he said instantly, a smile on his face. Jupiter sat down at the desk with him, waiting for him to finish typing the rest of his communication. "I'm good. It's scary, but I won't let them stop me now. I got accepted into the local state school. I got a scholarship to help cover tuition and an assistant on campus. Now, all I have to do is graduate. My mom is proud of me, but she is worried. You know how parents are."

"That is amazing. They are so lucky to have you in their program, and you will make an amazing teacher. I'm sure it is hard to have your mom worried about you when you are about to take such an important journey, but remember how lucky you are to have someone who cares so much about you."

"She's my mom. Of course, she cares." Jupiter had become so used to the pauses in response that waiting no longer felt awkward. The modifications did help, though, and the technology should continue to improve even more.

"Not everyone has parents that care as much as your mom does. Mine didn't like me all that much."

"Did they ever come around?" Sammy asked.

"I haven't seen them since I was sixteen," Jupiter said. "I had a teacher that had asked us our pronouns. She was young and cool, and I thought telling her I wasn't female would be okay. It was fine for the first few months of school until there was a meeting, and my teacher used my pronouns in front of my parents. It wasn't her fault, and I feel bad because she got fired because of some stupid law requiring her to tell my parents earlier."

"Your parents weren't okay that you are nonbinary?"

"No, they believed being trans was evil. They locked me out of the house. I saw them a few times while finishing high school, but just in passing. I never saw them after I moved away from college."

"How did you live if you weren't at home?"

"One of the students at my high school had two moms. One of the moms found out I was kicked out and let me live at their house while I graduated. They didn't understand the autism thing; they just thought I was weird. But they probably saved my life. But I don't think your mom is like my parents. She already has fought so hard for you, even if she doesn't understand that it isn't what you want her to fight for. I think she needs time to figure it out. It is stressful being an adult."

It made Jupiter feel good knowing they could help someone, even if it were just listening, even if it was just supporting.

"If you need anything, you let me know." After Sammy promised, Jupiter left to finish work before ending their day.

Chapter Twenty-Eight

Jupiter woke up to a knock on their door. A quick look at their clock showed that it was still seven in the morning, too early for anyone to bother them. Anxiety flared through them. Knocking was never good, and it should only happen if they expected food to be delivered. They were still wearing their pajama pants and t-shirt from yesterday, and they figured that would be enough to answer the door to anyone who thought it was a good idea to talk to them this early.

Another round of pounding started before Jupiter made it out of bed and the few feet to open the door. Outside was the manager. Jupiter tried to remember his name, but their brain was still tired, and it took too long. He stood in front of them, angry and impatient, but did not start the conversation.

"Jesus," Jupiter remembered. "Is something wrong?" Visions of autistic individuals being evicted flashed through their head. But they paid the rent on time, directly from their bank account. They were quiet, mostly. To their knowledge, no one had complained about them. But something had to be wrong for him to be here this early.

Jupiter looked out and noticed that a crowd had gathered. Adults stood outside, frozen as if stuck on their way to work. A mother looked up at the house and then covered her child's eyes as they walked out of the courtyard.

Jupiter looked around, trying to understand what the problem was. Then they saw the markings next to their door. It was bright red and looked a bit like a male anatomy. They stepped out of their apartment and saw that several outside walls were covered in at least three different spray paint colors.

"Die," it read right over their window. "Die Trans Bitch," was written on half of their door and the wall next to it. "Autistic Bitch," had been sprayed further down. "R—" was written repeatedly, and Jupiter realized that the word was spelled differently each time.

"Do you know who did this?" Jesus finally spoke. His words were sharp and full of anger. It took Jupiter a minute to realize that the anger was directed at them.

"No, why would I know anything about this?" Jupiter felt the tears threatening to come again. The words were almost comical initially, but that had given away the hate beneath them. The reality of knowing that someone hated you enough to go out of their way to call for your death hit them strongly.

"I know you are on that video that my children showed me. I saw you making trouble, and now you've brought it here to this place where we want to live in peace."

"I don't want this," the words sounded like a plea even to Jupiter. "I just want to live also. I don't want any of this."

"The police are on their way," he said. "They will get to the bottom of this."

"I need to put on some more clothes," Jupiter said.

"No," the manager said. "You will not be getting away before they come."

"I'm not going anywhere. I live here. I need to go put on some clothes to talk to them. I must contact my work and tell them I will be late."

It was a half lie, and it hurt Jupiter to say it. But they needed to tell Stanley. He needed to know what had happened, especially if they didn't make it to work today.

"Just be here when the police come," he said.

"I will," Jupiter said.

Jupiter went inside and closed the door behind them. Their apartment, which had felt so safe and separate from the outside world, now felt violated. They fell to the ground, unable to breathe. They felt like they were on fire and were coming apart. Then they remembered that they were not alone, not entirely. They remembered to focus on their breath, and when they were slightly more steady, they put on pants with actual zippers and buttons. Then, they grabbed their AR glasses and put them on. They typed out a message to Stanley with a link to a private video channel and started recording. They were trans and autistic, and they knew enough to be concerned when the police came.

When they felt ready, they opened the door and walked back outside. It had been at least fifteen minutes, and the police still hadn't arrived. Jesus was talking angrily on the phone, and a few residents were still outside watching everything unfold, but most of the crowd seemed to have gone about their day.

Jupiter turned and faced the graffiti. They let their eyes drift, not focusing on the words, but they wanted to make sure that it was all recorded, that there was evidence of what had happened. They couldn't say why. Maybe it was to remind Austin that not everyone was waiting this out behind locked doors with a security detail. However, they felt petty as they thought that. Except they were scared.

A message came through from Stanley.

> How did they know where you live?

> I don't know. I haven't even been going out, so I wouldn't get recognized.

> I will let Austin know and see what he can find out. Be safe, and let me know if you need anything.

The police showed up then. There were two of them, a Hispanic man and a white woman. As soon as they appeared, Jesus walked up to them, talking and gesturing to the wall, then he turned and pointed at Jupiter. As he spoke, the police paid attention to him, nodding their heads occasionally but mostly letting him talk. Sometimes, the male officer would interject with a question, but they seemed satisfied with whatever he said.

Jupiter stood watching; their body felt suddenly cold, and they wished they had put on a jacket even though it was already sixty-five degrees outside. Then, the male officer talked to the female officer, and she broke off and headed straight towards Jupiter.

"You live here?" she asked when she had walked close enough to reach out and touch Jupiter.

"I'm in 16," Jupiter gestured to their door, the one with the most graffiti.

"Do you know what this is about?" she asked.

Jupiter shook their head, the words frozen in their throat. They had never had good experiences with police, although they knew at least they had a better chance of walking away alive because of the color of their skin.

"Your manager seems to think you know what this is about."

"There was a video," Jupiter said. "Some people were saying hateful things online, and I asked them to stop. It became pretty popular."

"I think I've seen that one," she said. "They keep playing it on the news. So you're an activist?"

"No, I'm a gamer. I play games, and I help test them. Educational games for school kids." Jupiter knew the words were coming out fragmented, the stress of the situation jumbling everything up.

"You work at that elite school with all the autistic kids." It was a statement, not a question, so Jupiter ignored it.

"I don't know who did this," Jupiter said. "I'm not an activist. All I did was talk to some people one time. I've kept my head down since then. I've barely even left my house. No one should know where I live."

"Someone knows where you live." The officer made a vague gesture at the writing. "You'll need to work with your landlord to get this taken care of. Otherwise, he may press charges."

"Charges?" Jupiter asked. "I didn't do this. Aren't you going to find out who did?"

"We're going to write up a report." Jupiter noticed the male police officer had walked up to join them. "And we will increase patrols in the area, but there isn't much we can do in cases like this."

"There are video cameras." Jupiter pointed to the cameras that overlooked the courtyard. "They must have caught something."

"Even if they did work, we won't have time to sort through all of the footage to find something that wouldn't even help us to identify a suspect. We are facing budget cuts as it is," the male police officer said.

"This is a matter that you need to work out with your land-lord," the female officer said. "I can't imagine it will be cheap to pay all this off. Maybe he will let you work to repaint it instead."

"I. Didn't. Do. This." Jupiter paused after each word so they had time to process what they said. "I can't be held responsible for damages that there is no evidence I did."

"Looks like you are responsible to me," the male police officer pointed at one of the more explicit transphobic messages.

"What happens if they come back and try to hurt me?" Jupiter asked. "Isn't there something you can do when someone calls for my death?"

"Sure," the female officer said. "You can file a restraining order. You must ensure you know who you need to file it against."

"But you're not going to investigate to figure out who did this?"

The radios the officers were carrying started to go off, spouting code that Jupiter could only guess at. They both paused to listen. "We have to go," the female officer said. "Just make sure you don't keep acting up, and I'm sure you can work out some sort of arrangement."

Jupiter watched them walk over to the manager. They said a few words and then walked out of the courtyard towards their car, parked illegally, blocking the parking entrance.

The manager walked towards them. Jupiter thought about going inside and ignoring him but realized he would probably keep pounding on their door until they answered, so they stayed to get it over with.

"I will be calling a professional for an estimate. I will let you know when it is ready."

"Why?" Jupiter asked.

He stared at them like they were stupid. "So you can pay it."

"I. Did. Not. Do. This." they said again, ensuring they formed each word as clearly as possible. "Since I didn't do this, I am not responsible for any damages. I'm sure that the apartment has insurance or something to cover it. If not, use those cameras to figure out who did this and charge them."

"Pah," he said. "Those cameras don't work. But I am not paying for this. I will let you know once I have an estimate."

He walked away, pulled his cell phone out of his pocket, and started talking. Jupiter stayed outside for a minute, watching him walk away. They looked at the last few neighbors, who were finally returning inside now that the show was over. Then they went into their house and shut the door.

When Jupiter finally logged into work, Stanley was waiting.

"I saw the video," he said straight away. "They didn't even care. They looked at you like you weren't even a person."

"It could have been worse," Jupiter said.

"I know," Stanley said. "When I saw how they talked to you, I almost hopped on a plane to come down and help you. The only thing that stopped me was knowing I would be too late. What right do they have thinking some people deserve protection and others don't?"

Jupiter stared at him while he talked. They knew to fear the police. The statistics on deaths and beatings of trans and disabled individuals were staggering and often didn't even get media attention. But even with all that, they knew the privilege their skin color gave them. They knew the benefit that being more trans masculine than trans feminine gave them. What they didn't understand was how Stanley knew this fear at all. Most white people saw police as heroes, like the stars of the television shows they watched. Some were. Some protected everyone regardless of who they were, true heroes in blue. But even they were battling a system not designed to protect and serve. Most people didn't know the fear of finding out who would show up when the police were called. But it was obvious that Stanley did know because he was freaking out more than Jupiter.

"I'm fine," Jupiter said. "The police left, and I'm safely inside my house. I'm fine for now."

"I need you to go somewhere. Can you stay with friends, anybody?"

Jupiter hadn't told him about their family, but of course, he knew not even to consider it an option. "I don't have anyone." Before, that thought would have been enough to break Jupiter, but now they knew it wasn't entirely true. They had ASD, and these were their people. There just wasn't anyone who lived around them. "I just wish I knew how they found out where I lived. Hopefully, they get bored and move on with their lives, and something else will have their attention next week." But even as they said it, they knew how long hate could stick around.

"I'm going to talk to Austin. I'll have him put you up in a hotel or something. At least he can send one of the company lawyers your way. All this has to do because you work here, so it should be connected. What else do you need?"

"I just need to get back to work and think about something else."

Stanley left them alone then, but Jupiter couldn't concentrate on their work. Their mind kept flashing back to the words on the wall. *How could someone hate someone so much*, they thought, *especially someone who doesn't even know me?* But when your parents hated you, it wasn't all that hard to believe that strangers also could.

Chapter Twenty-Nine

When Jupiter woke up the next day, they tried to continue with their routine. More than anything, they needed the familiarity to combat the events of the day before. However, the events never left them completely. As they got up to eat breakfast, they kept expecting to hear a knock at their door telling them that there was more graffiti on the wall. When they put on their AR glasses to answer messages, their notifications were in the thousands. They tried to sort through them while they ate like they usually did, but these messages were far from ordinary.

There were offers for them to be paid to appear on news shows. Some were journalists asking for comments about the current political situation. Most were proclamations similar to what was pasted outside their door. After the first twenty messages, they removed their AR glasses and finished breakfast, staring at their white walls. They didn't get up and change, do their daily hygiene, or pick up their house. They didn't do any of the items left on their morning routine because it was now broken and would need to be rebuilt from scratch.

Still clad in their pajamas, they threw on their VR gear and went to work.

At least work was consistent. After logging on, they checked their daily tasks, briefly glanced at the staff chat, and entered the student chat. They had been trying to keep up with it to ensure they were okay. This morning, the chat was busy, full of various news clips and messages of concern.

> I hope they are okay.

One student said.

> Did you hear what happened to them? Someone came to their house. This is getting scary.

Another student said.

> I can't believe they posted their name on the news! And to not even use the correct pronouns. This is shit.

Jupiter became concerned about who was in trouble, so they selected the most recent video to watch. It was an uploaded video of a news broadcast, the bottom of the screen showing it was based out of Des Moines, Iowa.

"The instigator of the now famous online video has been iden-tified as Jupiter J'neii. Jupiter, also known as **XXX XXX**, had assault charges filed against h— when s— was seventeen years old when s— was living in Tennessee. It appears that s— now resides in California. There have been no further charges under h— new name. Much remains a mystery about this now infamous figure at the center of the debate of Austin technology and the rights of autistic people."

The clip ended suddenly, and Jupiter stood frozen. Stanley had come at some point while it had played, probably to stop Jupiter from seeing exactly what they saw.

"The rights of autistic people," they repeated. It wasn't the most important or impactful part of the broadcast. It was just the only phrase they could currently process. "Is there debate that autistic people shouldn't have rights? I mean, if they can question trans people having rights, I guess they can question autistic people as well. I should have paid attention more instead of running away."

"You were asked not to get involved," Stanley said.

"But it is happening all over again. Who am I kidding? It never really stopped. Only one type of person is allowed to have rights in this country."

"Are you ok?"

"I didn't assault anyone," Jupiter said.

"That was over twenty years ago. I wonder how they even found out about it."

"You knew?" Jupiter asked.

"We did a thorough background check before recruiting you."

"Then you know what happened?"

"Not the specifics. We saw the charges were dropped. The police report was mostly empty."

"I didn't do anything. I promise." Jupiter sat down on the edge of the desk. It felt like the whole world had started spinning around them.

"You don't have to explain anything." After waiting for permission, Stanley walked over to them and put an arm around their shoulder.

"I want to. I think you should know."

"Then I'll listen," Stanley said.

Jupiter looked down at the floor, unable to focus on anything as they haltingly told their story.

"I appreciate the family that took me in after I was kicked out, but I wasn't part of the family. Their daughter hated me, and Ms. Karen was indifferent towards me. Mostly, she ignored me like one of the puppies her wife adopted. I wasn't considered much more than a puppy. I'm not discounting anything they did. They didn't have to do anything at all. But I repaid them by not being at the house as much as possible. There were some places I would hang out sometimes; they let me do some work for money or food. One was this local bar. I was too young to be in there, but they were nice to me and let me do some cooking in their tiny kitchen. There was a cop that hung out there. They let him drink for free, he made sure they got help when they needed it, and he ignored things when needed.

"One night, the cop was waiting for me when I left the bar. I didn't have a key to the house, and they locked the door promptly at ten. If I wasn't there, I had to find someplace else to sleep. It was nine-thirty, and I was worried about making it back. I didn't realize he was following me until I got a few blocks away. He said his kid told him about me and that he would make me into a woman.

"I didn't make it inside in time, and I guess I was more banged up than I realized when I went to school the next day. A teacher sent me to the nurse who opened a case. The officer in charge of the case asked what happened, and I told him. Then he told me I was a liar because that was his friend. He filed assault charges against me. He told me that if I ever spoke about what happened, he would send me to juvie, where someone would kill a genderqueer kid like me.

"So I told him I made the whole thing up. They never filed a report, and after he was sure I would not make trouble, he eventually dropped the assault charges."

Stanley stood awkwardly, and Jupiter was grateful that he gave them time to digest everything.

"There has to be something we can do," Jupiter finally broke the silence. "Whatever Austin is doing is not working."

"You just have to trust him," Stanley said. "I have already contacted him. He is encrypting your ID so that they shouldn't be able to get through to you. You also need to pack up and get out of your house. You said you don't have anywhere to go, so go to a hotel for now. We will figure out a more permanent solution. Austin approved leave for you. You don't need to worry about getting paid, at least."

"I can't run away," Jupiter said. "What will that mean for the kids? Some are crossing protest lines to go to school. And I am running away?"

"Fine, then don't go on leave. Just get someplace safe. The schools have security, and Austin has contacted concerned parents about getting in-home support for the kids who need it. It isn't a long-term solution, but will get us through the current climate. The bottom line is that none of the kids are targets. You are. It is your face that is all over the news - your real face now. You need to get someplace safe."

"Okay," Jupiter said. "I'll pack and go to a hotel, but then I'm going to work."

Jupiter logged off and switched to their AR device to book a hotel reservation. With that done, they went and packed their belongings. They didn't have much in the way of luggage. They had moved down with just one duffle bag. They hadn't acquired much since, but the VR gear took up the entire bag. They finally packed some clothes in one of their canvas grocery bags. They looked around their house and decided to pack their gaming console as well. They wrapped it in some of the softer clothes and threw in their collection of game CDs. For good measure, they used the remaining space to pack up some food that would travel. They had done it, their entire life packed up in three bags.

They called for a ride service, threw on a beanie hat and a scarf even though it was eighty degrees outside, and left their house. There, tapped to their front door was a white envelope with "The Bill" written in large letters. Jupiter left it there and headed out to catch their ride.

The ride to the hotel was uneventful. They checked in quickly and traveled to their room on the 15th floor. Their window looked out onto the congested streets of Long Beach, but in the distance, there was a glimpse of the ocean. They weren't sure if Stanley was overreacting, but they were here, and it was the least they could do to make him feel better.

They unpacked all their clothes, connected their console to the hotel TV, and got ready for work.

Chapter Thirty

A loud, piercing sound cut into Jupiter's brain. They tried to ignore it, putting the pillow over their head, but it did not help. Then their brain registered the smoke filling their lungs, and they shot up in bed.

The room was lit by a bedside lamp they had forgotten to turn off. The air was a little foggy, but for the most part, it looked fine. However, it smelt like they were in the path of a raging forest fire, and fire alarms were shrieking outside their door. White flashing strobe lights flickered all over the room. As soon as Jupiter registered their existence, they became instantly overwhelmed. They had to get away. They staggered to the door. At the last second, they remembered the fire training drilled into them during elementary school. They returned, put on their shoes, and briefly touched the door handle. It was cool. That was good.

They opened their door and saw the people staggering in

robes and pajamas. Firepeople were helping, dressed in full yellow and black gear, they were knocking on doors and directing everyone toward the stairs.

"Is there anyone else in there?" one of the firepeople asked. The voice was deep and masculine.

"No, it was just me."

"Good," he marked something on a list and then looked up. "Head down the stairs to the right. They are safe."

He pointed in the direction that all the people were moving, and then he left to knock on a door. Jupiter felt dazed as they followed the crowd down the fifteen flights of stairs. The height was now becoming not only a disadvantage but a scary prospect. Once they reached the bottom, they were ushered into a makeshift tent with the rest of the hotel occupants, where they were told they would be checked for smoke inhalation and any injuries.

They stood on the side waiting while the first responders looked at those who appeared injured or were at greater risk. Two rescue workers carried in a stretcher with a person. They walked past fast, putting the person on a bed behind a curtain. All Jupiter saw was blood. They only knew the person was still alive because of the whimpering from behind the curtain. Jupiter looked at the people around them, the people who were safe. They stood and watched as an air of shock moved around the group.

Jupiter didn't know how long it took before they were seen by one of the medical staff. It could have been days or seconds; time had seemed stuck at the moment they left the hotel room. The person put a monitor over their finger and listened to them breathe with the stethoscope. They hadn't spoken at all, just stuck in their own timeless loop, working to ensure everyone was seen and safe.

"Excuse me." Jupiter's voice came out gravelly. "I just … Do you know what happened?"

They looked up then. They were feminine and Asian, probably around the same age as Jupiter. They had a tired look in their eyes, not shock, more like the end of an adrenaline rush.

"I don't know much. I know there was shooting and a bomb was set off. Thankfully, it wasn't a very good one, or things could have been much worse."

"Is everyone okay?" Jupiter asked.

"I can't tell you that." She looked away then and started putting the equipment back on its hooks. "You should be fine, but you should follow up with your regular physician."

"Thank you," Jupiter said. They got up and walked away but stopped at the entrance to the tent. They didn't know where to go. They were in an area cut off by some plastic tape. On the other side were reporters with lights on their cameras flashing in the early morning light. Briefly, they reminded Jupiter of the flashing strobe lights, but then the panic disappeared. They were nothing alike. Behind the journalists, there was a crowd of people. They all stood silently watching, and the sight of them witnessing this tragedy gave Jupiter a chill.

A police officer walked in front of Jupiter, and they flinched instinctively, but this was a disaster, and there were different rules than on the streets.

"Excuse me," Jupiter said, causing him to glance at them. "I'm not sure where I should go."

"You finished at the clinic?" He didn't wait for an answer before continuing. "There is a station that way where they will help you connect with family."

He pointed in the direction opposite the crowd, and Jupiter turned to look. "I don't see anything," they said, but he had already left.

Jupiter walked down the road in the direction that the officer had pointed. It wasn't a big road, just three lanes that were one-way. Jupiter couldn't help thinking about all the people who would start going to work in a few hours. They would find the road blocked and end up being late. Their bosses would yell at them, and after, they would hear about the bomb and talk about how scary it was for something to have happened so close to them. It was easier to think about those people, connected but removed, than how close they were to not waking up. If only this were a minor inconvenience on an otherwise ordinary day.

As they moved forward, they saw another tent set up. It was full of tables and chairs with some bottled water and packaged muffins and apples. People were sitting, the shock still fresh. Most were on their phone talking to people or texting. A young man, probably in his early twenties, had moved a chair away from the tent. He was sitting with his legs spread wide in sweats and a t-shirt, watching what sounded like news clips.

"The assailants entered the lobby just after one in the morning."

Jupiter saw a person with a clipboard and determined they must be in charge. They were moving back and forth between the tent and an area about ten feet away, separated by more plastic tape. People were standing there looking anxiously over at the tent of survivors. Unlike the people surrounding Jupiter, they all had taken the time to dress before they had left to find out about their loved ones. They talked to the person with the clipboard, getting momentarily sad but would go back to straining through the crowd, looking for some glimpse of someone they knew.

"According to one eyewitness, it was believed that two young men, now identified as Chad Bradworth and Eliza Woodson, entered with multiple guns, including at least two AK-47s."

Jupiter waited for the person with the clipboard to return. They may have some way of contacting Stanley, or there could be a way to get their portable device or glasses. Jupiter was more in awe of how many people thought to bring their phones amidst the chaos. If only they had remembered to grab their AR glasses off the charger.

"They were asking about the whereabouts of an individual believed to be staying at the hotel, the autism activist Jupiter J'neii. The front desk staff member refused to give out the room number and was shot. She is now in critical condition at Memorial Hospital. A struggle ensued, and during that struggle, a homemade bomb exploded. The security guard, whose name has not yet been released until the family has been notified, was killed on the scene. Eliza Woodson was also killed. Chad Bradworth was taken into police custody."

Jupiter froze, forgetting even to breathe. The person with the clipboard was heading their way. They looked around, trying to decide if they should run and hide, but no one seemed to have recognized them, at least not yet. They didn't want to bring attention to themselves.

"Shortly after, another incendiary device was set off in what is believed to be the residence of Jupiter J'neii. There has been no report on casualties. It is believed that it was a coordinated attack by the militia group The Red Haters, a group of known Neo Nazis."

"Name."

Jupiter tensed up, looking around them to see who had recognized them.

"What is your name?" The woman with the clipboard was next to them, awaiting a response.

"Oh, sorry," Jupiter mumbled.

"It's alright. It has been a lot for everybody."

Especially those who died or those struggling for life, Jupiter thought. The front desk clerk had saved Jupiter's life.

"It's. . . I mean, I'm Sara Jenkins." It was the first name that had popped into Jupiter's head, the girl from high school who had resented sharing her family with Jupiter.

"Alright, what room were you in?"

"1531." Jupiter decided it was best not to lie about that in the hope that they could get their stuff. Hopefully, they wouldn't check and connect it. However, they didn't know what to think anymore.

"Do you have someone looking for you, someone you need to contact?"

"I'm from out of town, Iowa." They said the first state that came to their mind. "I'm not with anyone. I need to contact my uncle, but I left my phone in my room. I'm sure he is so worried. Is there any way that I can get my phone out of my room?"

"I'm sorry, but the building hasn't been cleared for anyone to retrieve items. There is a hotline set up. We haven't received any calls for you yet, but I'm sure it is only a matter of time. He probably hasn't even woken up yet. If you know his number, you can call out."

"I don't remember it," Jupiter said, and the woman nodded her head like it was given, like it was the extent of everything wrong in the world that we no longer remember phone numbers. "Do you, by chance, have a tablet? He doesn't like the phone much and prefers email. I want him to know I'm safe when he does read about it in the news."

"I'll see what I can do."

She walked away then. The young man was still watching his phone. He had moved on to other videos of other newscasters, but Jupiter did not want to hear anymore. They also wanted to be far away if he looked up from his phone and put two and two together.

They looked around the area and found a chair mostly in the shade of a nearby building. The sun was still low in the sky, and most of the light in the area was provided by battery-powered lanterns on the table. Jupiter grabbed some of the food. Their stomach rebelled at the thought of eating, but they thought it would give them at least an excuse for squaring themselves away. People who did nothing tended to stand out now that the norm was looking at a phone.

Jupiter tried to appear calm, at least sort of calm. They knew there was some reason to be in shock, but now that the situation was hours old, people mostly returned to a version of their pre-shocked selves. Eventually, Jupiter opened up the muffin and ate it in small bites. People in the tent left, and others arrived. Jupiter didn't stare at anyone too closely, afraid they would recognize them now that things were calming down.

They had begun to think that the clipboard woman had forgotten about them or failed to get a tablet. They were deciding on the best way to walk away, making a plan in their head, trying to remain calm and not let their anxiety overwhelm them, when the clipboard woman returned with a tablet.

"I had to borrow it from one of the nurses, so when you are done, please give it directly back to me."

"I will. Thank you."

Jupiter opened up a website portal to their messages. They had logged into the website version of the school a few times for various reasons, and thankfully, the web address was easy to remember. They checked for Stanley, but he showed up offline. They tried to decide what to tell him when Jupiter noticed that police were walking towards the tent. They were coming slowly, stopping and looking at everyone in the area, and Jupiter knew they were looking for them. They needed to make this fast.

There was an attack. I'm safe for now but have no money or tech. I will hide at the beach until I figure out what to do.

They made sure to log out of their account and delete the address from the history before returning it to the clipboard woman.

"Thank you again. I appreciate it."

She looked at Jupiter as she took the tablet back, and Jupiter felt she recognized them. But it could also just be paranoia. When she walked away, Jupiter let out a small sigh of relief. They grabbed another muffin and bottle of water and made as if to stretch. Then they ducked under the plastic tape and walked calmly but briskly around the corner of the nearest building. Now, they just needed to make it to the beach undetected.

Chapter Thirty-One

J upiter sat pressed against a rock facing out towards the water. It was not a comfortable position, with the area being less a sandy beach and more a scattering of giant rocks that led to the water. They had felt exposed as they navigated through the tall buildings and towards the ocean. However, it was worse once they had passed them and neared the water. It was too open, just some grass and a walking path that Jupiter had recognized as the pier from one of the weekend trips they had taken to explore.

The area was still closed, but there were a few people around. Some were sleeping openly in the grass, and others were walking arm in arm for an early morning stroll. But none of them walked around openly in their pajamas, even if it was just sweat pants and a t-shirt. When they reached the water, Jupiter had hidden away as best as possible.

It wasn't actually a beach or the ocean. This was some inlet used as a marina. Behind them was the lighthouse, the light now dark with the morning sun. Across the water was one of the cruise ships, the decks still illuminated. In between was the water reflecting all the images from above. It was beautiful, and Jupiter wished they had spent more time in this area of Long Beach. Maybe they would have gone out more if they could have afforded someplace closer to the ocean. But that was the irony of this city. It was almost like it was two separate entities. One was full of pollution, cars, and people camped out on the sidewalks, just trying to survive. Then, this part of the city was a beauty unlike anywhere else that Jupiter had seen. Maybe some people could handle the disparity between the two, bringing the fractured nature into balance, but Jupiter couldn't.

They needed to move. This wasn't the beach, and there was no way that Stanley would think to find them bunched up between these rocks on the not ocean. But they weren't sure what way to go. They didn't have their glasses anymore, and it wasn't like they could stand up and start walking. Eventually, someone would recognize them. With that, the events of the night that they had tried so hard to forget came flashing through their mind.

Someone tried to kill them.

Someone killed other people while trying to kill them.

They saw the young women at the front desk refusing to give out their room number. They saw the bullet leaving the gun and flying towards her. Then they saw her fall back behind the counter. They visualized her still body, blood pooling out under her. It was more than what the newscast had shown. Their mind, so used to seeing the world as a moving picture, could fill in the details. This was a story that Jupiter knew would never stop haunting them.

The world would be waking up now, realizing what had happened in their city while they slept.

Jupiter was tempted to stay here, lodged between the rocks, trying to remain hidden from the world, but it wasn't a very realistic plan. The beach would most likely be filling up soon with tourists and locals alike. But they also weren't sure what to do. They had no money and no way to hide. California may be a collection of uniqueness, but even their sweats and t-shirt would stand out in the middle of the day.

They could go back to the hotel and turn themselves in. The police would take them in, and maybe that wasn't such a bad thing. Perhaps the police would protect them from everyone out to hurt them. But Jupiter had learned long ago that the police were not the divine angels of justice that the dramas made them out to be. If anything, they would be held in connection somehow, even though they were one of the victims. However, at least it would let Austin know where they were. If they had faith in anything, it was the power of his money and connections to get them to safety. He may have only met them a few times, but they were part of his company and mission. Except that Jupiter saw how he had handled the political situation. Things had not gotten better with his lawyers and strategists. There was only one person they wanted to reach, one they trusted to help them escape this situation: Stanley. But they had already left him a message. What else was there to do?

Jupiter stood up and went down to the edge of the water. They picked up some of the salty brew and used it to wash off the remnants of the prior night from their arms. Then they cupped some and used it to scrub down their face. They ran their fingers through their short hair and wiped off some of the dirt that had clung to their pants.

They walked a bit on the sidewalk. The area was still mostly empty, although it was starting to fill up. A Yoga class had gathered on the grass, and some tourists were taking in the morning by the harbor. Jupiter walked from the water up to the entrance to the aquarium. There were still a few hours before it was scheduled to open, but in the roundabout, there was a black Honda sedan parked. There was a pull in Jupiter's brain, some instinct telling them that this was not ordinary and they needed to go to safety.

"Jupiter, is that you? Are you ok?" The voice came from the direction of the car. Jupiter looked around, their eyes wide in fear. They could not see who had spoken. They couldn't see anyone. If someone were out to get them, this would be the perfect place to do so without anyone knowing. Jupiter turned, their first thought to go back to the yoga group to at least have witnesses to whatever was going to happen.

"Jupiter, It's Stanley."

"Stanley," the name slipped from their lips. Except it couldn't be him, not here in California. Then, they saw the form emerge from the car. He was lanky but not that tall. But the look of the hair and the eyes could be him. Jupiter found themselves walking slowly closer, trying to connect the figure to the avatar that was their friend.

"How are you here?" they asked.

"I booked a flight yesterday, as soon as you left for the hotel. I was worried. You didn't think I would leave you to handle this alone, right?"

The figure was not quite the same. There was something different than the avatar that they knew. But that voice they recognized. The words spoken so fast that one syllable blended into the next.

"But why are you here?" They gestured around them at the building with a giant whale and docks of boats for tourist rides.

"I took the earliest flight this morning. I was already on the plane when the bomb went off. They told us what happened over the intercom. I wasn't sure they would let us land, but somehow, Los Angeles was far enough away that they allowed it. I tried to drive to the hotel, but the roads were all closed. When I got your message, I went to the closest water I could find to where you were staying. I ended up here. I was waiting, trying to decide what to do next, when I saw you."

Jupiter stood, letting the information filter into their brain. They tried to find any holes in the story, anything to suggest that this man, their closest friend, and a stranger, was telling the truth.

"Jupiter, get in. We need to go."

Jupiter looked around. They weren't sure exactly what they were looking for. Someone hidden in the shadows to grab them? Maybe someone to jump out and tell them this was all a bad idea. But what they had was a familiar voice and a face that wasn't quite right, telling them to get into an unknown car. They did the only thing they could think to do. They got in.

Chapter Thirty-Two

S tanley sat facing forward, his eyes trained on the unfamiliar California freeways that were back-to-back with morning traffic. He had on a baseball cap, a well-worn blue one that did not have any symbols that Jupiter could see from their angle. He also had on a pair of dark black sunglasses. They looked cheap, like the type you would pick up from a gas station.

He didn't look the same as his avatar, although Jupiter had difficulty figuring out why from their angle. He looked softer; his jawline was a little less defined. He was also skinnier. Jupiter was used to his body skirting the line between muscular and plump, but in person, Stanley was thin, with only a little definition in his shoulders.

Jupiter knew that he would look different in person, at least conceptually. But seeing him this way felt wrong like the avatar was his proper form, not his flesh and bone body. It was the way they felt about themselves. Not that they thought anything was wrong with who they were, at least not anymore, but that it wasn't the person they saw inside themselves.

It was then that all the pieces clicked into place. All the comments that both Stanley and Austin had made. Stanley seemed to have more in common with Jupiter than he let on, but if he didn't want to mention it, then Jupiter would not either. After all, it was his identity.

"Maybe we should stop and get some food and let the traffic level off before we try to drive out of town," his voice cut through Jupiter's thoughts, bringing them back to the moment.

"I don't want to go inside anywhere." Even now, they kept themselves pushed back in the seat, looking forward, just one more person using a ride share to get to work.

"No, that wouldn't be a good idea. But I can go somewhere and pick up something. Maybe grab something to wear that will help hide your face a little."

"Is that what is with the hat and glasses?" Jupiter couldn't help the chuckle that came out of them.

"Not the hat," he said. "The sunglasses can help confuse facial recognition software. I decided it would be better to be safe than sorry. There are zealots all over, and I don't think you realize how big this story has gotten."

"I saw some of the videos from last night. People are getting hurt because of me."

"It may not help much, but the woman from the front desk will be fine. She pulled out of surgery. Mr. Austin has already taken care of all of her medical bills."

At the words, a pressure lifted off of Jupiter. There were others they knew, others whose faces they would learn and would haunt them for the rest of their days, but at least this news helped them to have the strength to continue.

Stanley was not making much progress in getting off the freeway. The cars were moving in small bursts, constantly stopping and going. There were only brief instances of gaps opening up that other drivers instantly filled. It was clear from Stanley's iron grip on the steering wheel and near hyperventilating breathing that he was not used to this type of traffic. Jupiter couldn't help either. They had only been on the California freeways a few times and never as the one driving. So they shut up and let Stanley focus on the road until he eventually found his way off. When he pulled into a gas station, his hands were shaking.

"So, I take it you're not from California?" Jupiter meant it as a joke, but they realized as it left their mouth that it probably was not all that funny.

"I live in Colorado. There is traffic, but nothing like that. Maybe if we wait until after eight, the freeways will clear up some."

Jupiter didn't have the heart to tell him that the freeways never cleared up from what they had heard; it just moved a little faster. "So you came out here to save me?"

"I was on my way as soon as you called. I knew trouble was coming. But, I didn't think it would come to this." Stanley took off the sunglasses and turned around to look at Jupiter. They saw how tired he was, like he hadn't slept in days. "I should have come out sooner or had Austin move you someplace safer."

"I wouldn't have gone," Jupiter said.

"I know you wanted to set an example for the kids."

"Well, wouldn't you?"

"Yes, but now you know you have to leave. You are a target."

"Yes, I can't sit around here letting other people get hurt for me. But I don't know where to go."

"That's easy. You can come home with me." When Jupiter didn't respond, he began to flounder. "You don't have to. We can find an anonymous place for you to hide out. Maybe rent a hotel room under the corporate identity. Although, that may not be safe either."

"Your partner, they won't mind?" Jupiter asked.

"It's just me, at least right now. I have a spare bedroom you can use, and we can get Austin to send you a new headset, one not tied to your identity. You can even go back to work if you want, not that you have to."

"That sounds wonderful. Thank you. I don't have ID to get on a plane, though."

"No way we can get on a plane. They are looking for you. They make it sound innocent enough that they are concerned for your welfare, but I don't quite trust it."

"Me either," Jupiter said. "But how will we get there then."

Stanley gestured to the car. "We'll drive."

Stanley went into the gas station, got them both some food, and bought Jupiter a pair of cheap sunglasses. They ate together in the car in the gas station parking lot. The parking lot was packed with cars filling up before work. Jupiter, who had now moved to the front seat, watched Stanley eye all the people wearily. "Is it always this crowded?" he asked.

As he said it, Jupiter realized that they had started to get used to the constant flow of people every time they left their apartment.

Maybe because they could escape it, it hadn't bothered them as much lately. But they still did not consider themselves a city person; getting away from the buildings and people made them happy. They knew many people loved it here, but they were not built for the city.

It didn't take long before Stanley became jittery about sitting in the gas station. He complained about being noticeable and moved to find somewhere else to park. He became lost in the traffic flow and ended up on the freeway. They drove through the stop-and-go traffic for hours. The car was silent, with Stanley even turning off the radio to focus on the unfamiliar road. Jupiter sat back, afraid to disturb him. The glasses didn't give them the sense of anonymity Stanley was going for, but they wore them and watched the city around them.

Finally, the traffic began to speed up. The roads were still congested, but now they could go long stretches without putting on the breaks even as they were traveling through steep, curving mountain freeways. There were still so many people, not a break in sight, and Jupiter couldn't help wondering how many of them were watching the news, hurting for the things being said about autistic people. How many had not even noticed?

Eventually, the traffic started to fade out for real. There were still cars, but there would be gaps between them now. The city seemed to fall off, and they were no longer surrounded by a parade of shopping centers. Then, even the freeway began to narrow, losing lanes until it became the rural passage that Jupiter was used to. With each shift, Stanley started to loosen. First, it was his grip on the steering wheel. Then he turned on the music and started singing. Finally, he was telling Jupiter stories.

"I knew Austin since he was a skinny boy in my sixth-grade classroom. By then, he already had learned to hate school, and who could blame him? He was bored by the curriculum and frustrated by all the rules he didn't understand. His teacher from the previous year told me he was terrible at math. He kept failing tests because he didn't show his work. He didn't know how to because his brain didn't slow down enough for him to take apart all the steps; he just knew the answer.

"I was the teacher that was given all the kids deemed to be a problem or to go nowhere. But that was only because I could see that most were not given a chance. Our educational system is not built to be flexible, and these kids all needed a little more. Not all of them succeed. I'm not a miracle worker, and there are just bad kids no matter what anyone tells you, but those kids tended to do just fine. Most of the kids I got were just different.

"I had him again when he was in middle school. I had been promoted to an administrator. I didn't want to leave the classroom. I just thought it would be better when," he paused then and looked at Jupiter before continuing. "Well, from when I transitioned. I wasn't out at work yet, but I was working my way towards it. He was such a smart kid. I didn't know how everyone else couldn't see it. I brought in this technology firm to do an assembly on technology innovation, and Austin latched on. Later, he told me that he managed to secure an internship with them in high school, and he eventually bought the company for more than they were worth to show his appreciation. We lost touch for a bit, then. I transitioned over the summer, hoping that it would just fly under the radar, and it did for about a month. But the backlash was too strong, and I got let go before winter break."

"That can't fire you because you are trans." It was the first time Jupiter had spoken since he started telling his story.

"No, they can't, at least not officially. But we both know it isn't hard for them to find other reasons to fire you, and they come away looking like heroes. I decided to move states. It was a bit too contentious where I was living. I decided it was best to start fresh. I was working for a charter school in Colorado when Austin found me. He said it only took him so long because he didn't know to look for a different name, and that was all he ever said about it. He told me about the school and hired me as the head administrator. That was four years ago."

By the time he was done talking, they had made it over the California border. They were both tired from not having a whole night's rest.

"I think we should stop and pick up some food," Stanley said.

"Do you think it is safe for me to be seen?"

"I'd say not yet. It is probably best if you stay in the car."

They stopped at a truck station, and Stanley picked up some food and got gas. He also picked up Jupiter a New Mexico hat, and a new t-shirt that Jupiter used the outside restrooms to change into. They stared at the doors before deciding to enter the men's room.

Jupiter tried to stay awake as they drove, but eventually, they found their head resting against the window, and they must have drifted off because when they woke up, they had stopped again.

"I just need to stretch and get some more gas," Stanley said when he saw Jupiter was awake.

"I'm sorry for falling asleep on you."

"It was good to see you sleep. You've been through a lot these last few days and needed the rest."

"What about you? Don't you need to rest? I don't know how to drive, so I can't offer to switch out with you. We could stop somewhere for the night, though." As they said it, their heart beat rapidly, and their breath caught.

"I think it is best to get back as soon as possible. I think you will be safe at my place, but the less people know where you are, the safer you will be. We should get there as soon as we can. It isn't that bad of a drive. We're almost halfway there now, and no more California traffic to deal with."

Chapter Thirty-Three

It was late in the night when they reached Stanley's home. They had driven straight through, only stopping for gas and food and the occasional rest stop that didn't look busy so that Jupiter could get out of the car. They were careful not to bring attention to themselves and drive through as fast as possible, which seemed to have worked.

Stanley's house was nestled in the middle of a subdivision with similar homes. It screamed, "I'm just like everyone else," that Stanley seemed to be trying so hard to convey, and for the first time, Jupiter realized that he might not have his life together as much as they thought. Maybe adulthood was just people pretending they knew what was happening. Some just did their pretending better than others.

Stanley pulled into the parking garage and escorted Jupiter to a guest room. Jupiter stared at the shower in the guest bathroom, trying to decide if it was necessary. With the realization that they still stank of the explosion, they showered. Then, they found sets of individualized hygiene kits stowed away, and Jupiter wondered precisely how many people Stanley took in. But they were happy with the new toothbrush and to feel mostly clean. They wrapped a towel around their body as best they could, the standard towel too small for their frame. And they wandered into the bedroom. They didn't want to put back on their clothes, but they also could not go naked in this strange bed in a house that belonged to their boss. Thankfully, Stanley seemed to realize this. On the bed was a pair of sweats and a T-shirt. They were a bit snug, but they worked even if they accentuated their chest in a way they were not thrilled about.

Finally, clean and dressed, they fell instantly asleep.

When Jupiter woke up, the TV was on. At least they thought it was a TV. They followed the sound towards the living room and saw Stanley staring frozen at the screen. Jupiter was mentally preparing themselves to see last night's events played on the screen, so it took them a few moments to look up. But when they did, the coverage was not what they expected. Instead, there was a news crew outside of what looked like a strip mall with a bunch of stores, except one was blackened with firepeople standing in front of it. The title scrolling on the bottom of the screen read "Autism school bombed," and Jupiter felt their knees buckle. They had to grab onto the back of the couch. The tears were already falling down their face, obscuring the rest of the broadcast, but Stanley woke up from his stupor enough to help Jupiter walk around and sit on the couch.

"Was anyone hurt?" Jupiter managed to ask.

"Yes," was all Stanley said before looking away. Jupiter realized that he had his AR glasses on.

"How hurt?"

Stanley looked at the floor, tears forming in his eyes, and Jupiter knew that one of their kids hadn't made it. Jupiter hadn't done enough to keep them safe. None of them had.

"Who?" Jupiter said.

"They haven't released the name yet."

"But you know." It came out as an accusation, but Jupiter let it stand.

"No one thought they would bomb one of the centers. Even still, most of them had been closed. Austin was sending help directly to the houses, but it takes time to find people and money, and it wasn't done yet. We didn't think they would hurt the kids."

"Who?" Jupiter asked again, but now they were certain they didn't want the answer. At the same time, they knew whose name would leave his lips before it was said.

"There were three students at the center. Isabelle's parents had already brought her home. Jacob wasn't there; they were driving in when it happened. The only student there was Sammy. He was there with one of the care instructors, Jessica. You didn't know her. She didn't have a VR interface. She didn't make it. Sammy is in critical condition."

The world fractured then. It was more than Jupiter could take, and their mind shut off while their body mourned. They curled up in a ball and started rocking. Tears fell uncontrollably as big, wracking sobs overtook them. Jupiter cried for Sammy and the front desk clerk, as well as for Jessica and their neighbors hurt in the bombing. It was for the despair that the world contained people who would do such things because they were different. Once Jupiter's brain connected again, it flashed to all the conversations they had had with Sammy, everything he had done to help those students he worked with—all his plans for the future. Maybe the world didn't see it, but Jupiter knew precisely what they had tried to take away. They only saw a kid who couldn't vocalize, who stimmed and didn't fit into their norms, instead of taking the time to see the kid who cared, the one who planned on being a teacher because the Austin School District had given him a chance, and he wanted to help so many other kids the same way.

By the time that Jupiter returned to themselves, hours had passed. The TV had been shut off, and Stanley was no longer in the room. Jupiter felt a fleeting shame to have shut down so completely in front of their boss, but then they thought about the grief again and had to get their emotions under control. They squished them into a little box until they could be properly processed later. They had things to do, and Jupiter knew that Sammy would understand. He would want to ensure that the world was adequately cared for and that all this madness ended. Jupiter would have to be the one to do it, and they would, for Sammy. First, they had to find Stanley.

He wasn't hard to find. He was in a room that was his office. Instead of a traditional desk, there was a VR rig. Jupiter watched him and realized that his setup was slightly different than theirs. While he may have been able to connect via the AVR, he did not seem to have the native ability to navigate. He had to physically walk in place, and his gloves seemed to have extra controls to help him navigate. They stopped and watched him, afraid of interrupting, but eventually, he seemed to sense their presence. He slipped up his visor and looked at Jupiter with concern.

"How are you doing?"

"I'm—" They were going to stick with the platitude they usually said, the generic *I'm fine* that everyone wanted to hear, but they couldn't do it, not today. They were not okay. They didn't know if they would ever be okay again. "I have a plan, and I need your help."

Chapter Thirty-Four

It turned out that Stanley had admin access to all the staff accounts. As a rule, he didn't use it, but he could log in as each user. It was a bit of an invasion of privacy when Jupiter thought about it, but it was also beneficial in this situation. He was able to retrieve the message that they needed.

At some point in the day, Austin sent a new device for Jupiter to use. They didn't realize how incomplete they felt until they slipped back on the AR glasses. They were tied to a secure account registered under a pseudonym and managed with the same protection Austin used on his account. Even still, they couldn't bring themselves to be completely comfortable. Maybe it was just because of everything that they knew they had planned.

Thankfully, it had been easy to import Jupiter's old avatar to the new identity, and they were once again moving around in the virtual space. Jupiter could finally breathe, at least a little. They wanted to check on the students, but Austin School District had been closed indefinitely.

Jupiter understood the reasoning, but it still hurt when the announcement played out. It felt like Austin was letting hate win, and while it was essential to ensure the kids were safe, closing down the school completely felt like giving up. Jupiter was not going to let that happen.

Jupiter spawned into a private world on VRSpace, one of virtual reality's more popular hang-out spaces. They had bought the room this morning and decorated it with two chairs and a table. They kept the walls a somber brown and everything else empty. It seemed appropriate. Their heart was pounding with anxiety, and they tried to keep their breathing even as they waited. They were one minute late, and Jupiter knew that wasn't abnormal, but it didn't stop all the thoughts flowing through their head. *This needed this to work. They were so out of their element.*

Finally, they received a request to join with the appropriate passcode. They checked the account and accepted the invitation. The show was about to begin.

"Let me start by asking why you decided to do an interview now after staying silent for so long?"

Their avatars were each lounged in the chair. Multiple recording drones were hovering above them. They were not actually recording but represented the angle at which the software was recording. It was a way to help remind them both that they were being recorded, and they were a common courtesy, unlike the streamer that had gone without them the day that Jupiter had started all of this.

"You just need to look on television to see what has changed. People's hatred is so strong that they have resorted to taking and endangering life. Why would anyone feel like they need to attack a school and harm a child?"

Stanley had gone through the possible questions that Jupiter would be asked. They had memorized talking points, things they wanted to say, and things they should not discuss. But they were still worried. Watching what came out of their mouth was not their strong suit.

"Did you know the student that was hurt in the bombing?"

"Out of respect to them and their family, I will not share any information. I, like the majority of Americans, am wishing for their recovery. The important thing to remember is that these actions are only the result of a few who are caught up in the hate. Autism is not bad or good; it is just one aspect of who we are, and most people know or are related to at least one person on the autism spectrum. The Senator created a campaign of hatred to win an election. It has caused innocent people to be harmed, like Crystal Hardlem, a hero to whom I owe my life. Her strength is why I am here. I will live every day trying to live up to her bravery." Jupiter became choked up then; the tears did not show in virtual reality, but they heard the way their voice caught when speaking.

"Did you know that she has an autistic brother?" The reporter asked. "They had watched your clip together repeatedly. When the gunmen asked for you, she knew exactly who she was saving."

Jupiter's eyes welled up under their goggles. They hit their thigh lightly, trying to get enough control to speak. "I didn't know that." Their voice broke, and they had to pause again. The pain was still so raw, and this had just made it worse. "I don't always have the right words to say," they started. "I don't think there are words that can express the emotions that her bravery has caused."

"How do we move forward from here?" the interviewer asked. It was the opening that Jupiter was waiting for.

"We need to move forward together as one world. Tomorrow night, we will be hosting a worldwide non-violent protest. The main gathering will be held in AVR and live broadcast to the main Austin Technology social media accounts. We also encourage gathering in virtual reality and in person. All we ask is that these gatherings are non-violent. We must show those full of hate that we are united, all autistic and neurodivergent people, as well as our allies. Working together, we can make the world a better place."

Chapter Thirty-Five

J upiter was sitting in the corner of Stanley's office on the couch cushions they had gathered. It wasn't as comfortable as their beanbag, but it was better than abandoning their physical form to the hard floor. Stanley was hooked up to his rig just a few feet away. But the pattering of Stanley's feet, the creaking of his rig, and even Jupiter's physical body were now distant memories.

They stood pacing backstage in a newly built outdoor stadium designed to hold thousands. It was the setting for the main protest, the one held in actual AVR, the one being broadcast all over the world. There were still thirty minutes until the rally was scheduled to start, and Jupiter stood behind the curtains, their hands clenched, too hesitant to look and see how many people had joined them. Even still, there were less than 100,000 headsets in production and perhaps 80 million autistic individuals worldwide. Only a fraction of those who needed to be here were here.

In-person protests had already been announced and organized in conjunction with others. Stanley had let Jupiter know about the ones in Los Angeles, Washington DC, and Atlanta. There were over 200,000 RSVPs across these three events, all because Jupiter had put the call out, and people had responded. But the one that had made Jupiter break down was the one being held in the town that Sammy lived in. When he got better … *he had to get better* … he would be able to see all the love and support from his neighbors. Jupiter just hoped that it was big and loud enough to outshine the hate that had occurred there. There were other cities, but Jupiter was too worried about speaking in front of all those people and started to tune Stanley out, pacing back and forth in the small space.

It was a conundrum. They needed people to show up. They needed their voices to be united. But Jupiter was so anxious at the thought of so many people waiting for their words. They were not the eloquent speaker needed at this moment, but they were what they had.

"You're going to be fine, kiddo." He had started calling them that since they had met. They were thirty years old and an adult, but it was nice, like they had formed their own family.

"Is it crowded?"

"Don't worry about that. All you need to do is pay attention to those in the room before you. Everyone out there is a part of this team, and they all have your back. If it is still overwhelming, then remember that this is virtual reality. You can always adjust your settings."

Jupiter laughed at that, but only because it was true. If they were doing this in the outside world, they would have to deal with all the sensory overload that came with it. Blinding lights, loud people, and itchy clothes. Now, they could control most of that with just a thought.

The stadium was not all that dissimilar from the concert that Jupiter had attended. Except now they would be the one on stage, and instead of begging for friendships, they were with people surrounding and supporting them.

Jupiter eyed the metal stairs that would take them up to the stage. From the side, they could see the open space they needed to occupy. Only a heavy cloth separated them from the crowd, but with their sensory input focused on their location, they could hear nothing beyond it.

Austin transferred in next to Jupiter, causing them to startle. He was dressed in his signature t-shirt and jeans. He gave Jupiter two thumbs up and, after waiting for permission, tapped them on their shoulder. "You made this happen. Remember that when you are up there, it will give you all the strength you need to make it through."

Then he was gone, sprinting up the metal stairs like it took no effort. He started talking, and Jupiter focused on how his arms moved just enough to capture attention but not enough to overwhelm the audience. Jupiter adjusted their input and began to hear the cheers of the crowd.

"He's had a lot of experience," Stanley said. "You don't have to mimic him. Just be yourself. That is who everyone is here to see."

Jupiter turned to him suddenly, that thought causing more anxiety than everything they had felt before. All those people were here because they thought Jupiter was someone special. They turned to pace or run, they weren't sure which, but Stanley grabbed their shoulders, squeezing firmly. "You have this."

Then they heard Austin finishing his speech. "Enough of me blathering on, now for the reason that we are all here. Sometimes you have the rare opportunity to meet someone who manages to change the world through their passion. Jupiter is one of the most passionate people I have had the pleasure of meeting. Whether it is about video games, education, or the students, they will work tirelessly to improve them. Many of you first saw them when they refused to stand by and let people talk about autistic people, our people," at this, a loud cheer arose from the crowd, "Be talked about with hate. It was hate that Jupiter had felt growing up being transgender and hate they did not want to see heaped onto the new generation. Kids that are their beautiful, authentic selves. What they did took bravery, and for any of you who fear public speaking, you know it also takes bravery to walk up on this stage, so please help me welcome Jupiter J'neii."

Jupiter took one last deep breath, grasped their hand to the handrail, and walked up onto the stage. They paused at the top, looked out, and nearly walked back down the steps. The entire area was full of avatars, crowded together in a way they knew most could not handle outside of AVR. Above them were a series of VR cameras centered on the podium and the crowd below. But Jupiter knew that they had to continue. There were a lot of people who were counting on what they needed to do today.

So they walked to the center of the stage, shook Austin's hand, and faced the crowd. Above them, their speech was being projected out into the air for only them to see. As they looked out, they focused on the words, trying to let the people fade into the background. They knew from practice that the speech would move location in the sky when they were expected to move their head and look at a new section. All the coaching that Stanley had given them on public speaking played on a loop, taking up all the space they had to think. Finally, they squeezed it into a tiny section of their brain and focused on just saying the first word.

"Good afternoon," their voice was shaky, but due to the microphone enhancement, it carried evenly to everyone in the crowd and was picked up as the primary audio on the broadcast. "I want to thank everyone for being here today. I know why you're here." Jupiter pointed to the crowd in front of them. "Like me, you are autistic or one of the few non-autistics that can use the AVR. You have seen the hate that has been poured onto our community. For many of you, this is not new. I do not mean that neurodivergent individuals have never been accepted by society, although that is true. I mean that our community is unique because it is inclusive. Autistic people come from every race, nation, and ethnicity. We come from families that are all neurodivergent and families where you may be unique. We have people from every gender and more individuals who, like myself, are trans and genderqueer. Many of you have already experienced racism, homophobia, transphobia, and sexism daily. You know hate. And for some, like our CEO Austin, being neurodivergent may be your only difference.

"I am not here to speak to what everyone has experienced because I will never know what it is like to be hated for the color of my skin. I am not here to be the voice of the autism movement. I am here to be one voice. One part of the conversation. I am here to call for all voices to be heard. We are starting a new social media campaign called The Faces of Autism. To join, use the hashtag TheFacesofAutism on social media." The hashtag appeared in the sky above the crowd, and Jupiter knew everyone could see it. They also knew that it was appearing across every social media channel. Right now, the website was being launched, and social media accounts were going live where a video that Jupiter had already recorded was being uploaded. In an hour, a video of Sammy in his hospital bed would be uploaded, and an hour later, a video created by the brother of the injured desk clerk would go live. There were 24 videos planned, one launching each hour through the next day. Afterward, they hoped the hashtag would take off, and others would join.

"To have your voice included, use this hashtag or go to theface sofautism.com and share your submission. Then, go to the website or social media channels and see the faces of autism. It is important that the world hears our voice and knows that we are here, we are important, and we will be heard. There are millions of autistic individuals in this world, and united, we can be louder than the hate."

The crowd started cheering at their words, and Jupiter saw a text message from Stanley showing them that the hashtag had already had thousands of hits, most of which were from worldwide protests. They took a breath and continued.

"Before I address why we are all here today, I want to speak to one more group of people. These are our families and friends, the autistic allies that have joined us today. I want to thank you. Thank you for being our advocate when we cannot, but even more so, for listening when we advocate for ourselves. Thank you for realizing that how we see the world differs from you, but it is no less important. Thank you for seeing us and supporting us.

"In high school, my parents found out I was non-binary. I was kicked out of the house, but a family took me in. I know that it was not easy for them. I don't even know if they knew I was autistic, but they did not understand me. Yet, they still gave me a safe place to sleep and helped me to get to college. I would not be here today without that support, so thank you. Family is not always who you were born with. Sometimes it has to be found. But family will stand by your side and support you unconditionally, which is more valuable than anything else. So a huge shout out to all of you today."

Viewports opened up in the sky, showing visuals of the different gatherings. The plan was to filter through the various locations during their speech. Jupiter didn't expect them to be cast into the AVR sky. It threw them off for a minute, but they focused and then blurred the crowd so that they could continue. They couldn't process what the audience was feeling towards their speech anyway. They only saw the reactions that Stanley kept sending them, letting them know they were doing well or translating the crowd for them. They knew that the next section of the speech would make or break the entire rally, so they continued.

"The truth is that even if you are not autistic, you are connected to someone who is. The estimates on the prevalence of autism differ, but even if you take the broad estimate of 1 in 100, there are over 80 million autistic people around the globe. Everyone is connected to autism, even if you do not know how. It could be someone you work with or that one friend who doesn't quite fit into your social circle as much as they try. It could be a sibling, a spouse, or a child. Or, in the case of Governor McTilen, yes, the same senator that advocated for the end of Austin School District and the hate you see around you today, it could be your nephew. A nephew who attends a private school that focuses on autism, whose tuition is directly paid for by Governor McTilen."

Even Jupiter felt the energy shift in the crowd at this revelation. It was massive, and unmuted participants gasped and started talking. The crowd became chaotic, and Jupiter worried that they had lost them, but Stanley sent them a message: *Give them a minute to process this, then continue.* So they waited for a minute exactly. When they resumed speaking, they did so loudly and clearly, cutting into the conversations and bringing everyone's attention back to them.

"I understand your shock at this situation. I hear your cries of frustration. But should it surprise us that politicians say one thing while doing another? Politicians have shown us time and time again that their primary concern is to gain and maintain power and money. There are exceptions, but they are exactly that: exceptions. You might be asking yourself why Governor McTilen was willing to turn his back on his nephew. In the law that he outlined, the one that would close down Austin School District and push students back into an education system that already failed them, he provided an exception that would only benefit the few lucky autistic people who come from wealthy families and can afford schools that would be able to qualify for this exception.

"But most of us are not rich. If we are employed at all, we are underemployed. We are underpaid and taken advantage of. We do jobs that most people will not do in various fields, and we are often given a higher workload with less financial reimbursement because we are typically compensated less than our more socially skilled peers. And those are the ones that are lucky enough to find employment. Did you know that paying us less than minimum wage is legal just because we are autistic? People justify exploiting our peers because they think it is in their best interest because it gives them purpose. Do you know what else gives them purpose? Giving them fair pay for the work that they do. Stop seeing us as less and see the value we have to offer in any situation. And I do mean all of us. Even now, I am not giving this speech to you alone. I cannot understand the crowd's mood or gauge your reaction. I have someone feeding that information to me as I talk, helping me succeed at an impossible task. Yet here I am, and others should be given the same tools.

"What does Governor McTilen gain from this campaign? Votes. His approval rating has gone up 15% since he started this hate campaign. Yet it took the lives of seven individuals, including two children killed in an explosion while sleeping. It caused Chrissy Jenkins to lose the use of her legs, a woman who saved my life when terrorists tried to kill me. It took the murder of Jessica Peterson, who died while protecting a 17-year-old autistic boy named Sammy Tims. Sammy and his classmates were working on a project to improve assisted communication for autistic individuals who, like Sammy, are non-verbal. He plans on being a teacher working with other non-verbal students, and the Austin School District gave him a chance at that dream. He has already been accepted into multiple colleges, all because he was given an opportunity.

"The sad truth is that public schools often cannot educate individuals on the autistic spectrum properly. Some autistic individuals thrive in public school, which is amazing for those who do. But others do not. Austin School District was created to give those kids a chance at an education. One that costs the taxpayers nothing. Austin School District is entirely funded by Austin Industries. Instead of creating a new space force, like other billionaires, Austin created a school to train the next generation of engineers, programmers, and artists. There were plans for two non-virtual schools to be opened next year and to increase the enrollment of the virtual schools by 500%. This still would only enroll a fraction of the kids that need this program, but it is a start. Instead, the program is closed because a senator wanted votes over children's safety. Is that the world that you want to live in?"

Jupiter paused after the last words, just like Stanley had told them. They looked out over the crowd, the faces too blurred for them to see anything, but letting them know that they cared, they were part of a whole. Then they turned and walked off the stage. As soon as they reached the bottom step and were hidden by the divider from the crowd, they collapsed, their breath turning into deep jagged puffs and their entire body shaking.

"It's okay," Stanley said, his voice not in the virtual world. Jupiter felt a blanket over their shoulders, their physical ones, and they dimmed the virtual world, putting on an augmented view of Stanley's office as they rode out the panic attack.

Chapter Thirty-Six

J upiter spent the next day curled up on the couch, watching the fallout from the rally. It was being covered on all major networks. An estimated 3.2 million people showed up for in-person marches across the globe. Another 200,000 attended the AVR virtual rally and others in VR. And another 10 million viewers watched the livestream of the event.

The video of Jupiter's speech was already nearing over 50 million views and still steadily rising.

It should have been enough to have changed the conversation. They should have won the war. Except as Jupiter flipped through the broadcast, all they saw were people calling them out for trying to normalize autism.

"This figurehead is trying to tell us to normalize a disorder." A middle-aged white man spoke in a frame on the TV. "They are trying to claim a unique culture and identity for a disability. We should be giving these people help, not trying to rally to write off this deviant behavior."

Jupiter flung one of the couch pillows at the TV, straight at his face. "Everyone refusing to help caused us to be in this situation," they screamed at the TV. Then they curled up in Stanley's comfiest blanket, flipping through the channels until their brain hurt.

It was the same thing on every channel. Men, and occasionally women, going on about how the autistic situation should be handled. There was not one openly autistic voice on any of the stations.

"They are missing the entire point," Jupiter said when Stanley brought lunch, takeout from a local Chinese restaurant.

"What is the point they are missing?" Stanley asked as he laid out their food on the coffee table.

"They still do not see us as people. The idea was to connect us, provoke empathy, and see that we may be different, but we benefit society. They are writing us off as worthless and broken and dehumanizing us. This is what led people to hate in the first place. If this continues, there will be more death."

"What do you plan to do about it?"

"The rally was supposed to stop it. It was supposed to unite everyone. It didn't even last 24 hours." Jupiter picked up the container of fried rice and started eating as they thought.

"Not everyone is as easily moved and instantly as devoted as an autistic heart. People need to know that the best and easiest move is to accept autistic people."

"The campaign was supposed to do that," Jupiter said as a few pieces of rice fell out of their mouth. "No one is even talking about it."

"Then how do you make them talk about it?" Stanley walked away, taking his food to his office while he worked.

Jupiter sat watching the TV and eating until they saw a face that they recognized. Tall Boy's face filled up the screen. He was sitting at a table across from one of the local news reporters.

"We've hung out a few times. They are really into music and asked to come to a concert with us. They are quiet and kind of awkward but nice enough. It is wild to have one of your friends become famous. It makes it hard to just hang out. I'm glad they're okay."

"Do you know where they are?" The news anchor was young, with long brown hair. Her face was serious like she was doing an important piece and not peddling in gossip.

"I mean, I wouldn't tell that. I would hate for them to get hurt." Tall Boy winked, and then the camera cut back to the main newsroom.

Jupiter sat trying to contain the anger that was building inside them until they realized that if the autistic voice were missing, they would need to make it available. They ran into the bedroom they were using, grabbed their AR glasses from the end table, and sent a ping to Austin on a direct line.

> Do you think you could buy advertising space?

As Jupiter waited for a reply, they began to pace around the bedroom, tapping the palm of their hand against their thigh. An eternity, or one minute according to the clock, later Austin replied.

What's your idea?

We need to show them who we are. We need to use the videos people are creating and pay for everyone to see them. Maybe then they will care.

Do you think it will be enough?

No, I don't. How is Sammy doing? Do you think he would be up for some publicity tours?

Chapter Thirty-Seven

S ammy was taller than Jupiter expected, like he had had a growth spurt and had forgotten or decided not to update his avatar. His arms and legs were lanky, and his face was starting to show the beginning of his adulthood, but Jupiter recognized the smile instantly. Jupiter instinctively looked him over, making sure that he was whole, and was happy to see that there were only some bandages left from the explosion.

Sammy raced up to Jupiter as soon as he noticed them. He wrapped Jupiter in his long arms and squealed in delight. Jupiter hugged him back, so grateful that he had survived and that his joy was still in this world.

His mother stood off to the side, clasping her hands in anxiety. She was shorter than both Sammy and Jupiter. Her hair was tight black curls, and she had dark skin like her son. She looked tired, like life had exhausted her to the point where she only knew how to run on fumes. They were in a private airport, everyone too afraid for the boy to fly commercially. Or Jupiter, either, not with their recent publicity.

It was weird to be back in California. The brief absence made Jupiter appreciate it more. But they knew now that this was not their home. They needed someplace with a little more space to breathe. But all that would have to wait, because they knew the next few days would be a nightmare, one they had created all by themselves.

"Are you ready?" Jupiter asked both Sammy and his mother.

His mother just nodded in resignation.

"Yes," Sammy said, his voice emitting from his AR glasses. "Let's go tell the world who we are." The new voice fit him more than it had in his younger avatar.

Sammy was never a quiet young adult, and he let his excitement show as they walked to the car. He let out squeals of excitement and let his hands move in joy. Jupiter found themselves smiling for the first time in days.

"You are all now familiar with Jupiter J'naii, the famous autism advocate. They are joined today by Sammy Tims, the student harmed in the bombing. First, I would like to say that we are all relieved to see you are doing well." The host was a white cis male with brown hair and a blue suit. He was the fifth one of the day, and they had all started to blend together.

"Thank you, Jim." Sammy made some motions with his hands. Jupiter knew that he was choosing a new template. They had created them together for each interview, and Sammy must have forgotten to switch between them. "Thank you, Robert," Sammy said.

"Yes, as you can see, Sammy uses an assisted communication device to speak. Jupiter, would you like to tell us more about that?"

"I think Sammy should tell us," Jupiter said.

"The device I use is integrated into the AVR technology. It has been a school project to update the technology to make it more effective in following the natural flow of voice communication. Although, I don't think anyone expected us to have to test drive it on national television so soon. We are programming it to have a more natural cadence, improved voice selection, and an easier inter-face for users of all ages to communicate more naturally." There was a slight pause as Sammy added to the recreated response. "Although, as you can see, we haven't ironed out everything yet."

The host gave a polite chuckle at the joke. "That seems like good work that you are doing, work that would benefit more than just autistic individuals."

"Yes, exactly," Jupiter said. "And it is work being done by students that other schools and society had written off."

"If you saw me walking down the street," Sammy said, "you would not think there goes an honor roll student who has been accepted into multiple teaching programs. You would think that is a weird black boy. I wonder if he is a threat. You may be disgusted by my stimming and cross the road to avoid me, or you may be afraid and call the police."

The host paused, uncertain how to respond, so Jupiter counted slowly to three in their head and came in with the rehearsed response to break the tension that Sammy created.

"That is why it is so important that we see the individuals behind the bill that Governor McTilen has proposed. It is why we launched The Faces of Autism campaign, a movement that has over one million videos using the hashtag."

"Yes, it has nearly broken the internet," the host seemed relieved at having been saved from directly responding to Sammy. "Jupiter, how do you feel being a part of this school and contributing to these students' success?"

"I love working with the kids. But I am a product of the school just as much as they are. Autism may wear many different faces, but we are all autistic. We all have our needs, which can vary depending on the day. Austin School District hired me after I was fired for being autistic."

"That is illegal," the host said in a horrified tone.

"Yes, it is illegal to come right out and say it. But it is not illegal to be fired for not fitting into the office culture, not being social enough, or having a day when you are not functioning as well as others. You can be fired for coming in late even if you work twice as hard and stay longer. You can be fired for not fitting into the exceptions of work culture - all ablest. Not just for people with autism, but all neurodivergent people and those with other disabilities."

"How do you balance the needs of the company with those of people with disabilities?" The host sounded like he was asking a thought-provoking question, not one that had been thrown at every disability advocate in every conversation, including all the ones that Jupiter and Sammy had already sat through earlier in the day. Jupiter dug their fingers into their thigh in frustration, reminding themselves that this wasn't about fixing the system. All they needed was for more people to hear their voices.

"That is a great question. Providing for the needs of those with disabilities often will benefit those who are non-disabled as well. Flexible workdays, automatic closed captioning, and even elevators and ramps cause no harm and benefit everyone. And if companies are not ready to diversify their talent, and if they take that stance, they are missing out on amazing people. At least let other companies do so."

"Do you think companies have a problem with that?" The warm lights of the studio were starting to drill into Jupiter's brain, causing them to lose focus for a few seconds. Thankfully, they had this script down and could find their place quickly.

"This bill, B345.6, is not just targeted at school or autism. It is legislation that will undermine the entire Americans with Disabilities Act. It will allow discrimination against disabled individuals in school, work, and even the community. It stops any organization from adapting to needs other than those who are non-disabled. Sure, it will only affect one state, but after it passes, other states will pass similar legislation, which will get pushed nationally. We have seen this happen over and over again. And why? The only reason for this bill is hate. Social programs such as Austin School District remove some burdens from an already overstressed and underfunded system. People are complaining and killing because we dare have programs that make the world functional for us, but they also won't create socially funded programs. They would rather that we just not exist, and if you read history, you will find that autistic and other disabled people were also victims of the holocaust. Ones that are often not even talked about."

"Well, you are passionate and articulate. How do you respond to people who say that you should not represent the entire autism community because you are too high functioning?"

Jupiter let out a sigh, closed their eyes, and refocused. They glanced at Sammy and, speaking their own nonverbal language, decided that he should answer first.

"We would start by saying that using functioning labels is ablest," he said. "Just because I am nonverbal and require assistance to get dressed should not deem me low functioning. It diminishes my intelligence and abilities."

"And just because you see me as verbal and professional in this setting does not mean I am not autistic." Jupiter joined in. "Just because you did not see the hours-long anxiety attack after the rally did not mean it didn't happen. I may have learned to mask—masking is a term we use for adapting everything about yourself to follow neurotypical rules—does not mean that I do not have my own needs, including the harm that masking causes."

"Functioning labels are used to diminish and divide us," Sammy said. "You may have heard that autism is not a spectrum. Instead, it is a wheel of different areas. Some days, we can excel in one area, and the next, we may have difficulty in that same area. Other areas may be a consistent area of need, and others may be a consistent area of success. Each person's need is different, but that does not stop us from being connected. But you are right. Jupiter does not speak for us all. They never said that they do. However, they were thrust into the role of advocate and have taken it up because they knew they needed to allow other voices to be heard. And you can hear them. They are your neighbors, co-workers, and even your children. If you cannot see the voices in your community, then go see them on social media." Sammy held his gaze directly at the camera as he spoke, and Jupiter was filled with joy that they had the pleasure of knowing this young man.

"But the most important thing," Jupiter said. "Is to support us. This bill has to be struck down. If it is not, then it poses a threat to everyone."

The interview ended shortly after, but there were two more left that day, eight interviews in 24 hours. By the time they made it back to the hotel, they couldn't even fake looking in the general direction of another person. They kept their eyes trained on the floor and their body clenched. When they finally made it safely into their room, they curled up in a ball on their bed and didn't move until morning.

On the flight back the next day, they sat frozen and silent, watching the movement of the world happen before them. Sammy, understanding their need, let them be.

Chapter Thirty-Eight

On the first day back in Colorado, Jupiter had spent the entire day in their bed. The guest bedroom had started to feel more like a home than their studio apartment ever had. On the second day, they woke up and managed to do their morning routine, but they felt lost at how to fill the day without work. They avoided the TV, afraid their last idea would not have made any difference. They didn't know what else they could do or if they had anything left in them to do it. So they sat on the couch staring at a blank TV screen.

"I think you should watch this," Stanley's voice startled them, bringing their thoughts back into focus. He picked up the remote, turned on the screen, and then directed a video file from his AR glasses to play.

The video was frozen on a teenage boy with fair skin and dirty blond hair. He was standing in a red plaid prep school uniform beside some trees. His arm was reaching out, most likely holding his phone up to do the recording. Then it started to play.

"My name is Timothy McMahon. Governor McTilen is my uncle. As you probably know, my uncle has put forth a bill that essentially would make it illegal for anyone who is disabled to gather together. He tells you this bill is to create equality, but we all know that is bullshit. The only exemption to this bill is faith-based organizations that meet appropriate guidelines. This exception will allow places like my private school, a Christian-based school that collects those of us whose families have money, to remain open."

The phone scanned to show a collection of at least twenty kids behind him. One was in a wheelchair, another with crutches, and a few were actively stimming their hands and fingers, moving to meet their sensory needs. All but one were white. Then the camera moved back to focus on Timothy, the other students still slightly visible behind him.

"Make no mistake. They are not making this exemption because we are esteemed members of their family. You will not humble them by reminding them that we exist. They put us here so they can forget about us; so we do not embarrass their careers. Some of us may be accepted back into the fold if we learn to hide who we are, but most will be cast off. Cast off with trust funds to keep us out of the spotlight. Well, except me. After today, I will no longer have my trust fund." Timothy held up a legal document to the camera. It was more a symbolic gesture, as nothing on it could be read. "One of the conditions of my trust is that I am never allowed to talk about being autistic in public."

"Oh, wow," Jupiter exclaimed. They turned and looked at

Stanley with disbelief in their eyes and then focused back on the video.

"A copy of this document has been emailed to every major news agency, along with this video. I am also including my lawyer's contact information to verify this. But I could no longer remain silent. I am proud to be autistic, and we want to stand with all our disabled siblings." The camera moved back as far as his arms allowed. The students were now holding handmade poster boards reading, "*We exist. We are not invisible.*"

"We are against the autism school bill," they all said in unison.

The video ended, and Jupiter stared off, trying to process what they just watched. Then, they turned the TV to a live news broadcast.

"We have authenticated the document that Timothy McMahon has sent out." The news anchor was one of the many that Jupiter had sat next to just a few days prior. "One caveat of receiving his trust is that he cannot publicly discuss his disability. By releasing that video, he violated that agreement and, as a result, will forfeit his trust. The big question is who created that trust. I am joined by Jacob Junkets, a lawyer who has followed this bill closely. What can you tell us about who created the trust?" the anchor asked.

"Timothy's parents are fairly middle class." The lawyer was a middle-aged man with rich, tawny skin and short black hair. "Governor McTilen inherited the majority of their family estate. Their parents seemed to have taken issue with their daughter's marriage. So, the trust was issued by the family estate manager, meaning Governor McTilen. The estate also pays for Timothy's schooling. According to sources, he was sent to the school eight years ago after a political opponent brought up his nephew's school behavior during a debate."

"How was the behavior mentioned?"

"It was suggested that Timothy was having tantrums at the school. However, as we know, meltdowns are a common reaction to overstimulation, and such behaviors would not be inconsistent with an environment not conducive to sensory processing issues."

"Oh, it sounds like you have some experience with this," the anchor said in mock surprise.

"I do. My oldest son also is also autistic. While I am not an expert on autism spectrum disorder, I am a parent who has had to learn to provide the best environment for my son. As a parent of a child who attends a school in jeopardy if something similar to the autism school bill were to pass in my state, I am strongly against it."

This was the first time anyone neurotypical had come out on the news firmly against this bill, and Jupiter felt their chest lighten at the change in tone.

They flipped through the various news stations where everyone talked about the video. Other advocates, who had been working for diversity for years, were brought on, not just autism advocates but for all disabilities. They were having frank discussions, but more and more of those being brought on were talking about how autism had impacted their lives. Their father was autistic, or their mother, maybe a nonbinary teenage relation, or their nephew. The conversation was no longer about an abstract group of people but real autism, actual disability, and the real impact that this law would have. Jupiter found themself tearing up.

It took until five at night Colorado time before the Governor called a news conference where he gave a speech trying to save his political career.

"Today, I sat down with my nephew and had a heart-to-heart with him. I explained how my motivation for introducing bill B345.6 was a genuine attempt at helping him and others like him. After our discussion, I did some introspection and realized that this bill would not have the effect I intended. It has already caused individuals to lose their lives and would cause others to lose the support that they depend on. We must come together to support everyone. We need unity, not violence. I will no longer be supporting B345.6 but will be working with all sides to create a bill that better captures the needs of this nation."

Timothy was nowhere to be seen on the stage, and the words were so full of generic pandering that it took Jupiter a minute to realize the implication of the speech. They won. The school could reopen.

Chapter Thirty-Nine

The reopening was done as quietly as possible. At first, students were required to log in from their homes or unknown individual locations. Austin supplied all the support needed to help families with what was required. Most parents had noticed the change in their children since the school was closed and eagerly worked to bring their students back. Other families were more hesitant, but by the end of summer, every student previously enrolled had returned to the school. Eventually, group sites were created. All of them remained unmarked to help minimize the chance of future violence.

The school expansion went forward. More than two thousand students were enrolled in the virtual school at the start of the next school year. Two smaller hybrid schools were set up that focused on art education. One of the schools was a boarding school, so students from across the nation could attend.

The waitlist for all programs had over ten thousand students, and a more considerable extension was planned to eventually allow every qualified student a place in the ASD school district.

Jupiter was no longer an educational consultant. They were instead promoted to Assistant Director, where their role became assisting Stanley with managing the entire school district. At least once a month, they found themselves back on the news or a guest on someone's online show. Although, they turned away most requests, as the interactions had never become less draining. Occasionally, they sat next to Senator McTilen, who had successfully won his election campaign. His nephew, Timothy, had transferred to ASD at the start of the school year, much to the Senator's disappointment.

Sammy started university, where his celebrity status made him instantly popular on campus. He already had a job offer for a teaching position at Austin School District upon completing his teaching credentials. But he was still active with the assisted technology club, which he joined as a volunteer as often as possible. Jupiter knew he would return to the school more often for student teaching. They stayed close, sharing an experience no one else could understand and a goal of helping as many autistic students as possible.

The assisted technology program was completed and put on the market, and all students working on the project received residual checks. Jupiter was surprised they received one and decided to turn their proceeds over to the new nonprofit organization The Faces of Autism, in which they were a board member.

It wasn't all positive. Jupiter still received hate messages. They were constantly misgendered on television. Their parents never reached out, trying to bridge a relationship, apologetic over the harm they had caused.

But they had a new family, one larger than they could have imagined. One that extended beyond the state of their new adopted home. They had decided to stay in Colorado, purchasing a house a few streets away from Stanley. They visited regularly, checking out each new boyfriend he brought home, but they also found other friends. They joined a gaming group in AVR that competed in tournaments to help bring awareness. They also found a group of friends in the outside world who were queer and trans. And others who, like them, knew that the power of friendship could be the strongest relationship. Especially when you would never have a traditional family.

When life became too busy or overwhelming, they called in sick, pulled out their gaming console, and returned to where they had first felt comfort in the world by pulling an eighteen-hour gaming session.

Acknowledgments

This book deals a lot with finding your place. As someone who struggles with social skills, this isn't something I am great at. Through writing, I have found my people. When I wrote my first book, I struggled to find anything to write in my acknowledgments. Now, I find I have so many people to thank. I have met some amazing people along this journey. Thank you for being here, even when I am awkward.

To all the readers who have taken a chance on my first two books and still picked up this one. Thank you! Hearing your feedback and encouragement is what makes the days of self-doubt bearable.

I want to give a huge thank you to my beta readers for this book. Specifically, Louise and Nadene. You made this book better. Also, thank you for my proofreader Chey. I am so happy to have been able to work with you again. Thank you for helping to spot what I could not.

Recently, I found the most fantastic audiobook narrator, Skye Alley. I never thought I would ever be able to have my books in audio, but you allowed that to happen. If that wasn't enough, you treated the stories with care and love, which has earned my eternal gratitude. If you are listening to this as an audiobook, then this is her voice. Didn't she do an amazing job? If you are reading this in print, I highly suggest you check out her work.

The online book community is such an amazing place full of wonderful people. I have met so many wonderful friends from Bookstagram and BookTok. This year, I started meeting friends on BookTube and BookThreads (is that the name?). You are my found family.

I also belong to two fantastic writing groups. NeuroSpicy is a group of neurodiverse writers. Thank you for reading through my work and always providing your perspective. You are all extremely talented. Also, to my fellow FSF Alliance members. I appreciate your companionship, all I have learned from you, and the community that you provide. Also, for all of you who provided feedback on the cover while I was freaking out - D.L., Amena, and Aura - I appreciate your patience and friendship.

As always, I am so grateful to my kids, who made me a better person just by their existence. A special shout out to my youngest, who hears all about my books, even when they would rather not.

About the Author

MJ James fell in love with books at a very young age. Books were the one thing in the world that made sense and provided constant companionship. MJ was diagnosed on the autism spectrum at the age of 24. After their diagnosis, they went on to earn a BA in Psychology and an MS in Developmental Psychology. They are the parent of three incredible humans.

Connect
www.MJ-James.com

Join my newsletter!

Instagram @MJ_James_Writes
TikTok @MJ_James_Writes
Threads @MJ_James_Writes
Youtube MJ_James Writes

www.ingramcontent.com/pod-product-compliance
Lightning Source LLC
Chambersburg PA
CBHW060910210726
48293CB00006B/2041